Final Part

Joe Brink Mystery Book 2

a novel by

Phil Bookman

This is a work of fiction. Names, characters, places, conversations, and incidents are products of the author's imagination or are used fictitiously, and are not to be construed as real.

Copyright © 2018 by Philip Bookman

All rights reserved. No part of this book may be reproduced or transmitted in any form or by any means, electronic or mechanical, including photocopying, recording or by any information storage and retrieval system, without written permission in writing from the author, except for the inclusion of brief quotations in a review.

ISBN-13: 9781729223079

Printed in the United States of America

First edition 2018

*"Have I played the part well?
Then applaud as I exit."*
Augustus Caesar
First Roman Emperor

Prologue

The couple was found by the maid, in bed in their penthouse suite atop the finest resort in Cancun. The morning sun poured into the huge bedroom like a spotlight focused on the bloody, mutilated bodies.

Though the murders had been particularly brutal, the motive, the police said, was robbery, specifically, jewelry. The narco gangs battling for supremacy in Cancun had branched out to preying on tourists, and the authorities appeared helpless to stop them. That the couple had been stabbed and sliced with such savagery was, they asserted, not noteworthy. Crazed violence was a hallmark of these heartless *matóns*.

The PR was abominable, especially after it was revealed that the woman was pregnant. To reassure guests, the resort made a conspicuous show of increasing security. This only made matters worse, and they gradually backed off, employing less obvious measures. It seemed that visibly armed patrols disturbed the guests even more than the prospect of becoming the victims of violent crime.

Phil Bookman

* * *

Stephanie had never intentionally harmed, let alone murdered, anyone before. She had been the neighborhood girl who nursed injured animals back to health. If not for allergies, she would have become a vet. Instead, she had found her calling in nursing.

She had also found and married Vern Cunningham, the love of her life. Much to the consternation of her clannish family, she followed him from the Midwest to Silicon Valley, supporting him as he went from one failed tech startup to another. They kept postponing having kids, waiting until he finally made it and they could afford for her to stop working, at least for a while, and start a family.

But it never happened. Instead, the man she thought of as her soulmate announced one day that he was leaving her. Their life together had become stale, he said. It was time for both of them to stop mistaking habit for love, he said. It wasn't her fault, it was him. The usual blather from a spouse bailing out.

Then he was gone. A week later, he called. Let's be reasonable, he said. A do-it-yourself divorce would save them each thousands of dollars in legal fees and the pain of the acrimony lawyers introduced into the process. The forms, complete with instructions, were all online. It would be the civilized thing to do.

Still in shock, Stephanie had foolishly agreed. Vern

Final Part

was between jobs and was asking for nothing from her. She could keep their apartment, furnishings, savings, everything except his old SUV. A month later, she was single, alone for the first time in her life. Her nearest family member was over 2,000 miles away. Lost and bewildered, too ashamed to go home, she threw herself into her work.

* * *

Six months later, Stephanie read about a hot startup that had secured a windfall of venture capital. The article was accompanied by a picture of the founders toasting their success. One of them was her ex.

She may have been naïve, but she was no fool. The bastard had been working on this startup all the while he told her he was out fruitlessly looking for work. Now free of her, he was suddenly wealthy. Stephanie consulted a lawyer, who told her she had no case. Yes, Vern may have hidden his prospects from her, but the startup company had not even been incorporated at the time of their divorce.

Stephanie tried to contact the bastard. He would not answer her calls, texts or emails. Then came the ultimate blow. Someone at work pointed out the wedding announcement. The bastard had remarried. There was a picture of the happy couple online. The bimbo was much younger. She was also conspicuously pregnant.

That was the moment that something about Stephanie changed. It felt to her as if her ability to feel compassion had died. She began planning her revenge. And it would most certainly include murder. More specifically, three murders.

Stephanie was at home in bed, over three thousand miles away, when Bimbo, Bastard and their unborn spawn were butchered. It was neither difficult nor expensive to purchase such services in Mexico.

Stephanie Cunningham did not sleep well that night; had not done so since the Bastard walked out. Curiously, it would be her last night of insomnia for quite some time.

Chapter 1

one year later

Living at home with your parents does not make for a good sex life. Especially when your girlfriend lives at home with her parents. And each of those houses is small with all the bedrooms and the one bathroom off the central hallway. Not much privacy conducive to romance.

And so it was that I had decided to take the big step of getting my own place. How, you may wonder, did a newly-minted private investigator, who had been in practice for himself less than a year, afford his own home in Silicon Valley, with its sky-high real estate market? Certainly not family money; there wasn't much of that. I had just invested my unexpectedly big payoff from cracking the so-called Perfect Murder, the case of rich and famous Rex Baker getting blown up during the live broadcast of his hit TV show, *Venture*

Capital Pie.

Rex's son Ryan had given me a fat bonus for solving that case and rescuing his mother from Rex's murderer. I mean fat as in six figures. Ridiculous, I know, but who was I to argue?

This bonanza was followed by a six-figure payment from a Hollywood production company for the exclusive rights to my take on the Perfect Murder story. I got paid that lofty sum for spending a week with a woman who called herself some flavor of producer, which in this case meant she was, as she told me, developing a "treatment" of the Perfect Murder. She was from L.A. and reminded me of one of my English teachers. Nice, precise, humorless.

During that week, I told Schoolmarm much of what I knew of the case while she took notes and asked lots of questions. She recorded our sessions, and I frequently referred to my case notes but gave her nothing in writing. We also visited what she thought were the key locations in the narrative.

Schoolmarm seemed happy enough with my tale. Her main complaints were that we in Northern California did not use "the" before freeway numbers—we called it 101, not the 101; we did not refer to the road along the coast as PCH or the Pacific Coast Highway, just Route 1; and, seemingly most alarming, the South Bay, where all the action took place, was nowhere near the Golden Gate Bridge, which she seemed to desperately want in a scene, any scene.

She was businesslike but friendly enough, and our time together was pleasant, mainly I think because I enjoyed talking about my adventure. After she flew home at the end of that week, I never heard from Schoolmarm again.

In any case, I suddenly had way more money than I or anyone in my family had ever had at one time. I had no idea how to manage this bonanza and couldn't turn to my parents for guidance.

I turned for advice to Nick Marchetti, a big-time financial guru I happen to know. After talking to Nick, I decided to use most of my windfall for a down payment on a condo in a new complex just a couple of miles from my office in downtown Campbell, California. I was acting responsibly. I was putting my money where I, impetuous youth that I was, would not be tempted to fritter it away, in a good, long-term investment, and taking advantage of historically low interest rates to get a fixed-rate mortgage I could afford.

Afford? Hah! It wasn't as if I got a paycheck I could count on. One thing I had learned since I became self-employed was that the need to meet monthly commitments helps focus your mind on generating income. You know, the opposite of outgo. Income good, increase; outgo bad, decrease. Words to live by.

Anyway, I was finally going to be out of the family

home. All grown up and independent. Adulting like crazy, as my friends say. And it was not just the privacy issue. Age 30 was not far off. It was time.

Chapter 2

I had just returned to my office from signing a mountain of paperwork at the title company and wiring hundreds of thousands of dollars out of my account. I was a homeowner!

I sat at my desk thinking about cash flow and generating the income I needed to pay all my new bills when Boomer Montana walked in. My expression must have belied my concern about my new responsibilities.

"You look awfully happy, young fella," said the grizzled Willie Nelson look-alike.

I told Boomer my home ownership news and he congratulated me.

"Your day in the Valley?" Boomer lived in a remote cabin deep in the woods in the Santa Cruz Mountains. He came down into Silicon Valley once a week to stock up on groceries and such.

"That, and I need your help with something. Couple of friends of mine are dead. Car wreck. They say it was an accident, but I don't think so. And it sure as hell wasn't suicide."

That did not leave many choices. "You're thinking

homicide?"

Boomer nodded solemnly. "I am."

"Tell me about it."

"Sharon and Tom Mayfair. Known Tommy since we were in 'Nam, where we blew things up together. He was drafted, served his two years and got out. We didn't stay in touch while I did my 20 years, but when I got out, I looked up some of my old Army buddies.

"Turns out Tommy had gone to college, gotten married and moved out here from somewhere back East. Did something with computers. We reconnected, and since then I saw him maybe once a month for lunch and a beer or two, a couple of old goats swapping war stories and lies.

"Anyway, yesterday, I call Tommy to set up lunch. Phone's no longer in service. I poke around, find out they're both dead.

"Seems one morning, a jogger noticed what looked like a fresh path where something had crashed through the brush off the shoulder up behind Lexington Reservoir, got curious, spotted what looked like a car under the water, called 9-1-1. They were both inside the car, DOA. Cops decided the car had gone off the road sometime during the night. Called it an accident."

Lexington Reservoir is in the foothills of the Santa Cruz Mountains, just east of the freeway where it starts its climb out of Silicon Valley heading south towards

Final Part

the beaches of Santa Cruz. What Boomer called "up behind" was the rugged, rural terrain where Alma Bridge Road wound around the east side of the large manmade lake.

"I read about that in the newspaper. Why don't you think it was an accident?"

"Tommy was in the driver's seat. Thing is, Sharon wouldn't let Tommy drive anymore. Still had his license, but he was starting to get a bit forgetful and his mind would sort of wander, so she did the driving. And even before that, he had stopped driving at night because he had trouble seeing in the dark."

"How old was he?"

"Like me, in his 70s. Look, no way Tommy would drive, especially when they're together, especially that road after dark. And what the hell were they doing in the middle of nowhere at midnight?"

"You tell the cops that?"

"Tried. Gal just paid me lip service. But I could tell she was going through the motions just to get me out of her hair."

I had just signed up for a 30-year mortgage. I had insurance, utilities, association dues, lots of property tax, and who knows what else to pay. I had office overhead. I needed to devote my time to generating real cash income, not taking on a *pro bono* case, even for my friend Boomer. I told myself it was time to grow up and be responsible.

Phil Bookman

"Let's get started," I said.

Chapter 3

The good news was that my new condo came with major appliances. The bad news was that it was otherwise bare.

Except for my big-screen TV, I wasn't taking any of the furniture from my room in what I now thought of as my parents' home, where I had lived for as long as I could remember. Looked at with the fresh eyes of a homeowner, my tiny old bedroom looked like it was for an adolescent. I was acutely aware that it had not changed much since I was a teenager; the student desk, dresser, bed and nightstand would be left behind.

My mom, ever the optimist, said she was turning my room into a guest room that could do double duty as a playroom for grandkids, "Should I ever be so lucky." Ever the pessimist, it meant, at least for now, it would change little, though the drawers and closet would be emptied. "Just in case," I heard her whisper to Dad at one point.

As part of the purchase deal, I had gotten my choice of paint colors. My girlfriend Anna and I had decided on white for the ceiling and windows, with something called Swirling Smoke, sort of a light tan-gray, for the walls. We had chosen the shade of brown stain for the hardwood floors, selected kitchen and bathroom tiles and fixtures, and so forth. I found the whole exercise exhausting but was happy that Anna had definite opinions where I had none. I was also glad someone else had done the painting and other finishing work.

Anna was another payoff from the Perfect Murder case. Her brother, David, had been arrested and charged with murdering Rex Baker in front of millions of live *Venture Capital Pie* TV viewers when the device he was demonstrating as part of his startup's pitch to the VCs exploded. Anna hired me to prove David innocent. After I did, we started dating.

Anna was jazzed about the prospect of furnishing my three-bedroom, three-bath place from scratch. Her enthusiasm dampened when I revealed my budget. She agreed when I said no to going to garage sales. I had decided to leave my old junk at home; I didn't want someone else's. My place was so new and spiffy, I wanted to go with that look. Anna said that wasn't exactly a look, but she got what I meant. She pointed out that getting all new furnishings on my meager budget would mean going slow. "I think this will take a while, Joe."

So first, the necessities. The kitchen, bathrooms and laundry room needed stuff, but not furniture. That was our Saturday morning activity. Anna knew I needed

Final Part

things I would never have thought of until I was in the middle of doing something and realized I didn't have potholders or spot remover or a plunger. Stuff like that.

After we unloaded the haul from Target out of my overstuffed Prius and refueled with burgers at Greasy Jack's, we headed to IKEA, armed with a tape measure and measurements and photos of my master bedroom.

I was ready to buy what was shown in the second exhibit. As is. It was not to be.

"You'd be in and out of here in a half hour if you were on your own, wouldn't you?" Anna seemed incredulous, but it sounded like a good plan to me. I had much to learn. I discovered that the first pass, as Anna called it, was for scouting, not purchasing.

We were having the requisite IKEA couple's argument until I gave in to the notion that furnishing the bedroom meant more than buying a bed and dresser. Actually, I first gave in to the notion that Anna knew what she was doing and I was clueless. I thought I was furnishing; Anna was decorating. I learned that I needed nightstands, lamps, a chair, window coverings and a big mirror. Plus a bedroom carpet and bathroom rugs. "The floors get cold at night," she explained.

And then there was bedding. As in more than sheets, pillows for your head and a blanket. I needed a duvet—*oui, oui*—and accent pillows. Speaking of sheets, I asked Anna, "When did they start counting threads?"

"You're lucky you're cute, Joe."

I was also informed that the bare walls would need some art, but that could come later in the decorating process. I thought that with a mirror and my TV, the walls would be covered enough, but also knew I was now a passenger on the interior decorating train.

I got with, or gave into, the program. When we selected the last item, it was after 7 p.m. We were wiped out, but returned to christen my new place, making love on a blanket on the floor. Then we grabbed a pizza at MySlice, I took Anna home and went back to my parents' house. I had not quite yet moved out. One more night.

* * *

Next morning, Anna came by and we put all my stuff, mostly clothing, in our cars. There was a lot less than I had imagined there would be. Or, as Anna put it, "You are definitely not an accumulator." I decided to take that as a compliment.

My things in the garage were from when I was a kid. An old bike, a tent and sleeping bag, miscellaneous sports gear, and other items in cartons that I had not touched in years. I decided to leave them, promising myself I would come back and get rid of the junk, which my mother was calling memorabilia, sometime in the future.

My friend Sally Rocket joined us at my new place at

Final Part

10 a.m. IKEA delivered shortly thereafter, and we began the assembly and positioning process. Sally, who also came with her own tool box, was very good at assembly. *Note to self: buy some basic tools.* Something Anna had not thought of.

Anna was very good at positioning. And repositioning. I was very good at taking direction, holding things, moving things, hanging my clothes in the closet, and organizing the drawers in my newly assembled dresser, which, I was informed, needed lining first. So that was what the big roll of paper Anna had insisted we get at Target was for. In time, all things are revealed.

I was careful to leave room in the dresser and closet for things Anna might want to bring over and keep in my place, a conversation we had not yet had, but she had already left herself a couple of empty drawers in the master bath vanity. In the private eye business, we call that a clue.

The cable guy came around noon. I got TV, phone, Internet and security service from them. I would finally have a phone that did not answer "Brink Investigations." My number would be unlisted, and I planned to be very careful about giving out my home address. I had learned that a private investigator should only use his office address, lest disgruntled clients or others he encounters—meaning pisses off—decide to visit him at home to settle a score. To the outside world, I resided at my office.

When Cable Guy was done and my TV was positioned and working in the master bedroom, I felt I had moved in, though I kept that thought to myself. *Note to self: need big TV for living room.*

I set up some folding chairs around a folding table in the dining area. My laptop and printer went on a folding table in the bedroom that would become my home office.

I made a lunch run for sandwiches. When I got back, the women were discussing the bed assembly and positioning with two men. I was introduced to Jonathan Wright and Charles English, who were in the process of moving into the condo down the hall from mine. It took no great detecting for me to realize they were a gay couple. There was nothing swishy about them, but they way they related to each other made the couple part obvious; the gay part thus followed by keen deduction.

The guys said they had just dropped in to say hello and were heading out for lunch. They complimented me on the progress I was making on my place and my excellent choice of decorators, meaning Anna and Sally.

As we were eating lunch, Sally asked, with what I was sure was feigned innocence, "What will you do with the third bedroom?"

A while ago, when I had been discussing with Anna why three bedrooms would be a better investment than two, she had uttered the word nursery. We had quickly

Final Part

glossed over that *faux pas*.

"Nothing, for now," I said. But Sally was looking at Anna and dropped the subject. Some kind of female telepathy thing.

By mid-afternoon, the master bedroom, phase one, was done. I had to admit it looked great.

"It looks great," I admitted. "How can I thank you two?"

"Paris," said Anna.

"Vegas," said Sally.

"Unless those are new local restaurants, you'll have to try again."

After Sally left, Anna and I messed up the bed.

Chapter 4

Santa Clara County Detective Nicki Nguyen owed me a favor. I was pretty sure she would have helped me out even if I hadn't once given her a couple of Warriors tickets, but it didn't hurt.

"You know I can't let you look at the file or anything in it, Joe."

"I know."

We were talking on the phone. It was better than me coming into the Sheriff's Department and people seeing her with me and the case file.

"But that file somehow found its way onto my desk. Let's see. Looks like a routine auto accident. Sedan with two elderly passengers, Sharon and Thomas Mayfair, husband and wife. Went off Alma Bridge Road, probably sometime after midnight, through some brush and down a steep drop into about twelve feet of water. Windows were open, so the car filled up fast. Airbags deployed, and they were found with their belts still on. Cause of death: drowning."

"You're thinking they couldn't get their belts off and try to get out?"

Final Part

"I'm not thinking about this case at all. But in general, I think if a frail old person gets walloped by a collision with the water and pummeled by airbags, they don't have much of a chance. I think you only have about 20 or 30 seconds submerged before you pass out."

"Autopsies?"

"No unusual findings."

"Who was driving?"

"Looks like it was Mr. Mayfair. Why?"

"My friend says Mr. Mayfair no longer drove. His wife did all the driving."

"He had a current, valid California driver's license, Joe, and was listed as a driver on their auto insurance. Anything else?"

"Not yet."

"When you get something more substantial, let me know."

She said when. I knew she meant if.

* * *

Other than the county park that includes the reservoir, a fire station, and a cluster of gated, multi-million-dollar homes, there wasn't much but wilderness along Alma Bridge Road.

The park closed at sunset, hours before the Mayfairs car went into the lake. But perhaps they were visiting one of those homes that evening. I gave the tedious chore of contacting the residents, who I have found rarely just sit at home waiting for an investigator to call on them, to Boomer, who decided it would be a good week to get in a little fishing in the reservoir while he checked them out and, as he put it, scouted around.

The freeway, state route 17, heads south out of San Jose through the little towns of Campbell and Los Gatos before it climbs into the Santa Cruz Mountains. I got off at Alma Bridge Road. Once past the parking lot on the east side of the reservoir, the area became heavily wooded, forming a natural barrier, and it would be hard to avoid the trees between the road and the water. I finally found where the accident—I was still thinking of it that way—occurred. There was a small opening in the trees at a sharp bend in the road where the dry brush still showed tire tracks. There was an orange traffic cone lying on its side, probably left there by mistake.

I called Boomer, who was on his way down the mountain on the other side of the reservoir, and told him approximately where I was. A few minutes later, he pulled off the road in his pickup and parked behind my Prius.

We looked over the scene together.

"Doubt they were coming from those houses," Boomer said.

I nodded agreement. The path of the tracks through

the scrub showed that they must have been travelling towards the houses, not away, in the middle of the night.

There were no tire marks on the road, no signs of braking there or on the ground. It looked like they took a straight path to the water through an opening in the trees about 15 feet wide.

"Sort of threaded the needle through one of the few spots where you'd miss a tree," Boomer said.

"They could have just missed the turn," I said. "It must be dark as hell here at night."

"I live in these mountains, you don't have to tell me about dark. I'm telling you, Tommy would never have been driving. If Sharon couldn't drive for some reason, they sure as hell wouldn't have come out here, heading away from the freeway."

"So you said. My cop friend said that wasn't much to go on, not enough for them to pursue."

"Well, it's enough for me. Still in?"

"Yeah, Boomer, I'm still in."

* * *

I left Boomer to do his scouting, got back on the freeway, and was in my office 15 minutes later. I called the County Medical Examiner's office, saying I was a friend of the Mayfairs and wanted to know when the memorial would be. After putting me on hold briefly, a clerk cheerfully told me, "Their son was here last week and authorized us to release the bodies to a funeral home. We did. That's all we know."

That was the first I had heard of a son. I came away from the call with his name, William Mayfair, along with the name of the funeral home. I called them. After a brief delay, I got the director. They had already held the memorial service which, the director revealed, had been "very private." I pressed him about who else attended; he sounded nervous and said he could not recall.

* * *

"I got a phone call about that matter we discussed. The guy said he was a friend of the family."

"Tell me the whole conversation."

"I can do you one better. I recorded it."

"Can you play it now so I can hear it?"

He could. He did.

"Nice work. Destroy the recording."

"No problem. When do I get my other $500?"

"I'll drop it off tomorrow."

"I'll be here."

Chapter 5

Boomer and I were sitting in the sunshine at a table in front of the bakery downstairs from my office. Boomer said the coffee and donuts were his treat. I think he felt guilty about me working on his case *pro bono*. I was enjoying a glazed donut, all the better to get a sugar rush of morning energy. "How'd it go?"

"The short version is, I got nothing. None of them had ever heard of Sharon and Tommy, let alone had them over that night. What I figured."

Boomer had canvassed all the homes along Alma Bridge Road. It had taken him the better part of a week, because, oddly, the residents had not been hanging out at home, waiting for him to drop in.

"But they talked to you?"

"Sure, why not? I'm just a harmless, sad old coot wondering why his friends were in their neighborhood the night they died."

It's damn hard to get people to talk to you when you're a private investigator. I was used to getting doors slammed in my face and sometimes worse.

Boomer's peculiar charm and simple story, especially with no mention of suspicion of foul play, had worked better than anything I could have come up with.

"What do you know about the Mayfairs' children?"

Boomer's brow wrinkled in concentration. "One son. Can't remember his name. One time, we all got drunk out on their patio. Out of the blue, Sharon says, 'You're lucky you got no kids. You think they're a blessing, then they crush your soul.' Tommy changed the subject. Next time I saw him, he mentioned that the boy was born after they had given up on having kids, one of those surprises. Didn't turn out so good, I guess, 'cause they didn't have any more. Anyway, we never spoke about him again. Why'd you ask?"

I looked at my notebook. "William Mayfair, age 30. Busted in New York several times for using and dealing, did some time on the last dealing charge. Recently got out of a treatment program as a condition of early release. Cops called him when his folks died, he came right out, sent the bodies to a mortuary for cremation, seems to have started acting as executor of their estate."

"You really are a detective, aren't you?"

"I'll tell you more, but it'll cost you a jelly donut."

Donut and coffee refills procured, I filled Boomer in. I had traced William Mayfair to an address in Queens. The place was a cheap residential hotel. He had been employed as laborer at a warehouse a few blocks away.

Final Part

"I called his boss, said I was a detective from California. I may have left out the 'private' part. Guy was pissed off, said Billy had quit with no notice, gave him some cock-and-bull story about his parents getting killed in a car accident in California. Left him shorthanded. I told him the story was true and asked him what Billy was like. He said he came to work on time and sober, did what he was told, stayed out of trouble. That was all he cared about. I gathered the employee performance bar was set a bit low." I closed my notebook. That was as far as I had gotten.

"What now?" Boomer said.

"Let's go for a little ride."

* * *

Wedged between the tony towns of Los Gatos and Saratoga, Monte Sereno was a postage-stamp sized hamlet with a population of about 3,000, most of whom lived in luxurious single-family homes on large, wooded lots. There was no commercial or industrial zoning, no shops or stores or downtown. The narrow lanes had no sidewalks and looped and meandered haphazardly. Think sleepy, rich, bedroom community.

I had looked up the property records and, in case it might already be on the market, the real estate listing. The Mayfair house was a tiny, three-bedroom, two-bath ranch on a two-acre lot. Built in the 1950s, the couple had bought it in the '70s. Unlike most homes in the area, it still had its original small footprint. It was listed for sale for an astonishing $3,999,000.

I parked in front of a 'For Sale-By Appointment Only' sign that showed a big photo of a beaming Suzy Lou, the real estate agent.

Boomer and I walked up the narrow blacktop driveway that led to the empty carport on one side. It was connected to the front door by a flagstone walkway. There was a cleared strip of landscaping maybe 20 feet wide out front, just some sorry-looking grass and a few tired shrubs. We did a 360 around the house. A tiny, barren patio of concrete blocks was out back, just outside the kitchen door. There was also a small vegetable garden that was suffering from severe neglect. Otherwise, it was a weather-beaten house in the woods, mainly tall pines and redwoods.

As we went around, Boomer looked in through some of the windows. When we got back to the front, we stood facing the house. "Looks like the place has been stripped inside," he said. "There's nothing in there. No furniture. No rugs. No drapes. Picked clean."

A female voice shouted, "Sorry, guys, you're too late."

We turned to see the real live Suzy Lou taking a 'SOLD' sign out of the trunk of her Lexus. As we walked over, she hung it on hooks under the big sign with her smiling face on it.

Final Part

"I guess we won't be making a bid," I said.

"Sold for 250k over the listing," Suzy said, flashing the same dazzling smile as was on the sign. "Four-point-two-five million. A couple in high tech, what else? Cash deal, would you believe? Took less than two weeks." She gestured to the tiny house. "Now they'll tear it down and build a mansion. What a crazy market. But maybe I can help you gentlemen find something else."

"No, ma'am," Boomer said. "I'm just an old friend—was a friend, I guess—of Sharon and Tommy. Just heard they passed. Came by to sort of say good-bye. Some good memories here." He extended his hand. "Name's Boomer Montana. This here's my young friend Joe."

Concern creased Suzy's forehead. She put a hand on his arm. "I'm sorry for your loss, Mr. Montana. Have you spoken to Billy?"

"Never met the lad," Boomer said. "And please call me Boomer."

* * *

Ten minutes later, the three of us were seated in a little sandwich shop around the corner from perky Suzy Lou's office in Los Gatos. It was one of those trendy places that featured every manner of grilled cheese. Which was okay with Boomer, since they also served beer.

"You said it would be a teardown. That means the land is worth over $4,000,000?" Boomer said incredulously, after we ordered.

Suzy nodded. "Two flat acres. Old-growth trees. Prestige address. Close-in yet private. These properties rarely go on the market, and when they do, they're gobbled up." She sounded like a real estate ad.

"There sure is a lot of money in Silicon Valley," Boomer said, shaking his head in amazement. "You must be getting rich."

"Don't I wish. My problem isn't demand, there's plenty of that. It's supply. For all the noise about the cost of living driving people away, no one seems to be selling in this area. A lot of them go to rental to take advantage of stepped-up basis. I hate to say this, but we wait for people to die to get inventory."

Boomer winced.

Again, the hand on his arm. "Sorry, that was insensitive," Suzy said.

While we ate lunch, we gently pumped Suzy for information. I let Boomer, who seemed to have charmed Suzy, do most of the pumping. By the time lunch was over, we had learned quite a bit. It seems that real estate agents do not necessarily respect client confidentiality as scrupulously as private investigators. And Boomer was getting damn good at this. I, too, deserved some credit. The white wine I kept topping off for Suzy had surely helped.

Final Part

Note to self: look up stepped-up basis.

Chapter 6

The second-floor space above the bakery and fro-yo shop was divided into three suites. Sally Rocket's self-defense studio occupied the entire rear side of the building. Across the hall, with scenic views of bustling Campbell Avenue, were my small office and Mr. Vu's larger suite. Mr. Vu was a financial planner whose clientele consisted mostly of aging Vietnamese boat people like himself.

Sally barged in just as I was opening up the sport's section of the morning paper. She plopped herself down in a guest chair and announced that Mr. Vu had just retired. "He's stopped seeing clients. We need to give him a retirement party."

I was about to tell Sally that it was a great idea, when a man walked through the open door.

"We'll talk about it later," I said to Sally. "I have an appointment." She smiled sweetly and was gone.

* * *

"Thank you for seeing me on such short notice," my

Final Part

guest said, taking the chair Sally had warmed up. He had called a half-hour ago and asked to see me.

"Brink Investigations prides itself on prompt customer service," I said. More accurately, I had a very flexible appointment calendar. As in, none at the moment. Not that I wasn't gainfully busy. Between insurance fraud cases and odd jobs for my former employer, Kowalski-Wu Investigations, I had enough work to keep me going. Barely. And then there was the Mayfair case I was working on as a favor to Boomer. As in free.

His name was Dell Chamberlin. Looked to be in his early 30s. We had already done the call-me-by-my-first-name thing. Sitting across from me, he sized up my spartan office. He seemed unimpressed by my minimalist furnishings, which fell into two sometimes overlapping categories, used and cheap. Or, as I preferred, functional and serviceable. Perhaps my location over a bakery and a frozen yogurt shop, across the hall from Sally Rocket's self-defense studio, had not met his expectations.

"Aren't you kind of young to have your own detective agency?"

"Alexander the Great was in his 20s when he conquered the world," I said.

"Nice comparison." *At least he hadn't said, "Delusions of grandeur."*

"What brings you here today?" I had been practicing my open-ended questions.

"I have a problem I think you could help me with."

I smiled sagely, as if I solved people's problems all the time.

"I'm a lawyer. Got my own practice and I need an investigator. My old guy got to be an old guy, and he's retiring."

"Aren't you kind of young to have your own law practice?"

Dell smiled and gave me an appreciative nod. *"Touché."*

"How did you come to me?"

"I read about what you did on the Perfect Murder case. And, of course, you're the Accidental Hero." He looked around. "I also see you have, um, low overhead." Meaning he figured my rates would be low.

A few months ago, I had been on a motel stakeout, getting the goods for a client on his errant wife, when two little kids who had been kidnapped walked up to my car. I then subdued their abductor by braining him with my camera when he came charging at me in a rage. The *San Jose Mercury News* reporter had dubbed me the Accidental Hero. It had been my 15 minutes of fame.

The notoriety from the rescue did little to increase my fledgling business, though it had brought Anna to my door when her brother was arrested. She had read in the newspaper article that I worked cheap, not exactly the best reason to pick a PI, but she and her family

Final Part

had limited means, as in just getting by. I had swallowed my pride and taken the case, with surprisingly good results. You can never tell how things will work out.

He asked about the kinds of cases I had been handling. I told Dell it was mostly insurance work recently. I also mentioned the Mayfair case, but only in general terms. Then I asked about him.

Dell Chamberlin's story was that of a promising Santa Clara University law graduate who was on the rung just below partner in a big San Jose law firm when his drinking problem gave his would-be partners pause. They made it clear that he was no longer partner material, and he was dismissed, though it was couched in "your talents may fit better elsewhere" terms.

Dell did what lawyers do. He sued. He claimed many actionable grievances, he said, but mainly that, under the Americans with Disabilities Act, his employer was obligated to accommodate his illness, and had been remiss in not providing alcoholism counseling and offering employer assistance treatment referrals.

"They work you to death for years in the mad chase to make partner, then drop you like a hot potato when the stress gets to you. Short story is, I won. Got a decent settlement. Of course, then no one would hire me, so I had to go out on my own. It turned out to be a good move. I'm sober and plan to stay that way. The practice is doing well, and I got the bastards to pay my startup costs."

I smiled. Dell probably thought I was happy for him, getting to start his own law firm and all. I was thinking happy thoughts all right, but they were about the prospect of adding another income stream. I also liked how he called his business a practice. The word had class.

"How big is your firm?"

"I run lean and mean. I have a secretary and a paralegal."

Lean and mean indeed. But I was leaner.

"Just one more question, Dell. What kind of law do you practice?"

"Yes."

Huh? Oh. I nodded. "I see. Kind of like me. Whatever the client needs."

He pointed the index finger of his right hand at me. "Whatever the client will pay for," he corrected.

Ah, lawyers and their precise language.

"I did criminal defense at my old firm. It's still what I specialize in, but I'm building my practice and can't afford to be too choosey."

I nodded knowingly.

"I assume you're interested in my proposal?"

"I am."

Dell seemed satisfied, as was I. We shook hands. I would be Dell Chamberlin's contract investigator, which means I would work on cases as assigned. It was

Final Part

a good addition to my practice, and I was already anticipating a steady stream of new income.

Chapter 7

earlier in the year

Sharon Mayfair heard the doorbell well enough, but it took her a while to put her book down, slip on her shoes, rise from the chair and carefully walk across the living room to the front door. Not many people came to the door in their quiet neighborhood. Those that did often rang a second time before she got there. Whoever it was this time already had points for patience.

The peephole in the door was useless. Neither Sharon nor her husband could see clearly enough through it without their glasses any longer, and neither of them had ever figured out how to position their bifocals to see who was out there. So they kept the security chain on. Sharon opened the door a crack.

"Can I help you?" Sharon heard the timidness in her own voice. She didn't like the vulnerable sound of it, but it was how she felt.

Final Part

"Hello, Mrs. Mayfair. My name is Stephanie Cunningham. I'm from the county health department, here to see how you and Mr. Mayfair are getting along. I wonder if I can come in for a few minutes."

"May I see your ID, please?"

"Certainly," Stephanie said. "It's good to be careful who you let in." She held her county employee photo ID up to the crack.

Sharon examined it. It said the lady was a public health nurse. She undid the chain and Stephanie Cunningham entered the Mayfair home.

In a matter of seconds, the two women evaluated each other. Sharon saw a pleasant-looking woman who appeared to be in her mid-thirties, maybe 40. Tall and thin. Tasteful makeup. Businesslike hairdo and outfit. Low heels. Small pearl earrings, no other jewelry. No rings.

Stephanie saw a white-haired woman who looked her age, which she knew to be 75. She wore a white top, tan pants and what used to be called sensible shoes. A touch of lipstick. No jewelry except for a craft-fair necklace and a wedding ring. Intelligent, curious eyes.

The door opened directly into the living room. The kitchen was to the right. A hall to the left that must have led to the bedrooms. Thomas Mayfair, also 75, was sleeping in one of a pair of easy chairs in front of a gas faux-log fire, a book open on his lap, snoring *softly. He wore a blue collared shirt, tan slacks, and had a full head of white hair.*

"Tommy, we have company," Sharon said, nearly shouting. She shook his shoulder.

As her husband stirred, then roused himself and, without comment, headed for the bathroom, Sharon offered her guest tea. She went into the kitchen and Stephanie sat on a loveseat at right angles to the chairs, facing the front door, taking in her surroundings.

The first thing Stephanie noticed was that the place smelled clean and fresh, normal. No mildew, none of the musty, closed-in, not-completely-clean odors that often accompanied the elderly.

The house was neat, clean and tidy, but looked lived-in. A short pile of newspapers was on the floor next to Tommy's chair. A half-filled glass of water was on the coffee table in front of Sharon's chair, and a shawl was draped carelessly across its back. But no junk, no empty food containers or dirty dishes. Things were in their place, but not compulsively.

It was a small room, but did not feel closed-in. There were a few miscellaneous pieces of furniture and some knick-knacks, but not too many. You could move around in here without watching your elbows lest you break something.

And there were books. Except for the TV mounted over the fireplace—the only furnishing that looked like

Final Part

it was less than a decade old—the walls were covered in bookshelves, filled with books of all kinds. Which made complete sense. Sharon Mayfair was a retired librarian. Cunningham noted approvingly that the books had not leaked out of the shelves; none were stacked on the floor or on furniture.

The only photos she spotted were an 8x10 wedding pose of the young Mayfairs next to another obviously recent 8x10, which, according to the inscription on the frame, had been taken on their 50th anniversary. That was it. No family shots. No photo of their son at any age.

Sharon returned with a tray containing three matching cups, a teapot, milk, sugar and teaspoons. She set it on the coffee table as Tommy returned, and Sharon introduced him to their guest; he appeared to just realize she was there. After the tea was served, Stephanie explained the reason for her visit.

Stephanie Cunningham worked for a county program for isolated, at-risk seniors. At risk of what? Bottom line, high healthcare costs. Which meant high costs to Medicare, which paid for the program. The idea was to provide some in-home support to help seniors stay in their homes and reduce those costs. However, people balked at being called isolated or at-risk, and the mercenary angle was a turn-off, so the program was officially described only in vague, positive platitudes.

"*This is a free government program for folks on Medicare. My job is to be sure you're doing okay and getting the services you need. If you agree, I'll drop in to check on things from time-to-time. There's no cost to you.*" Stephanie had learned to stress the free part right away.

Tommy smiled. Sharon looked skeptical. "How did we get chosen? You can't possibly do this for everyone on Medicare."

The answer was all about isolation. Somewhere in the bowels of the Department of Health and Human Services in Washington, a computer algorithm calculated what was called the social isolation index, the SII, for each Medicare client. The higher the SII, the higher the projected lifetime Medicare costs, or PLMC. And controlling PLMC was the new Medicare imperative. It was not about quality of life or quantity of life; it was about cost of life. But Stephanie was not about to tell her clients any of that.

"I don't know," Stephanie said with a pleasant smile. "I'm just assigned clients." Time to change the subject. "Here, let me show you."

It was brochure time. Stephanie handed Sharon and Tommy a colorful, glossy brochure full of pictures of smiling seniors of various races, some single, some couples. In each photo, they were chatting with a much younger, helpful looking person. Everyone looked healthy and thrilled with whatever was going

Final Part

on. There was a limited amount of verbiage, and what there was consisted of meaningless, upbeat marketingese. The emotional message was, sign up and these earnest young people will help you old folks look as blissful as the ones in the pictures. It had been developed for HHS by an ad agency that also worked with pharmaceutical companies.

Stephanie thought that, like his wife, Tommy looked to be in good health. His eyes were clear and intelligent, and, now fully awake, he followed conversation appropriately and was engaged. It was just that his memory was fading.

* * *

Immediately after Stephanie Cunningham left, Sharon checked up on her. She knew better than to call the number on the card Stephanie had given her. Anyone pulling a scam would be sure to have that number answered as if it were a government office. Instead, she called the main Santa Clara County government number.

After working through several bureaucratic levels, Sharon reached a woman who answered the phone, "Senior Support Services. How can I help you today?" It was the same number as on Stephanie's card. The woman confirmed what Stephanie had told the Mayfairs.

Phil Bookman

Stephanie Cunningham was legit.

Chapter 8

Where was Billy Mayfair?

I know, I'm a detective. I'm supposed to be able to find people. But William Mayfair, who apparently went by Billy, was in the wind. I didn't know if he had intentionally vanished, but my keen investigative mind was suspicious.

It seems that after he was notified by the police of his parents' deaths, Billy sprang into action. He quit his job, flew to San Jose, identified the bodies and arranged for them to be cremated.

Three days after the deaths, Billy walked into the real estate office closest to his parents' home. Suzy Lou happened to be at her desk and she soon had a new listing.

Billy told Suzy he had already taken everything he wanted from the house and asked her to arrange to have everything left removed—he didn't care what they did with the contents—and have the property prepared for sale. He wanted it on the market right away. They agreed on an asking price. He left all the details to her. They agreed to leave the utilities on and he said his next stop would be the post office to stop the mail.

Suzy had verified that Billy was in fact the successor trustee of the Mayfair Family Living Trust, which held title to the property, and was also executor of the estate. He had all the paperwork, including their wills, the living trust and death certificates, which she reviewed. She noted that he was the sole beneficiary of the estate, and wrote down the name of the local attorney who had prepared the estate planning documents. Just to be on the safe side, she later called the lawyer's office and confirmed that she had seen the most recent documents and no probate was required.

That was the only time Suzy had seen Billy Mayfair. All other contact was by phone and email. I had tried to wheedle his phone number and email address from her, but she balked at giving us those details.

Suzy also told us that Billy Mayfair was polite, well-spoken and well-groomed. He wore a dress shirt, sport coat, slacks and loafers, and was driving a BMW convertible with dealer plates. It was a 6 Series, she said, and looked new. She was a little jealous because she had recently looked at the same car, but a sexy, red convertible was not practical in her line of work.

She also explained that it was not unusual in her business to handle a sale with little in-person contact with the seller. Her dealings with Billy had raised no red flags.

Final Part

* * *

I wanted to find Billy Mayfair because he was the only one who seemed to benefit from his parents' deaths. We also had no other leads to follow.

Boomer had spent a couple of days chatting with the Mayfairs' neighbors. As with those who lived by the reservoir, the main challenge was catching them at home.

The Mayfairs had lived in the sort of neighborhood where you knew your neighbors to say hello, maybe saw them walking a dog, but didn't socialize. Sharon and Tommy were the old couple who had lived there forever and kept to themselves. No one knew them well. No one had anything bad to say about them. They were quiet, no barking dog, kept their place looking decent, rarely had company, gave good candy at Halloween. Perfect neighbors.

Googling the Mayfairs proved fruitless; they had no online presence. No Facebook or other social media accounts. Nada.

* * *

I was getting up to leave when a guy in coveralls and carrying a stepladder walked into my office.

"Excuse me. I'm doing some work on the vacant space next door and need to get into the ceiling on your side of the wall."

I understood. The guy was working on the space Mr. Vu had vacated. When Sally and I installed our security system, we had spent some time running cables through the space above the suspended ceiling. It contained a maze of cables, conduits, ductwork and pipes.

"I'm on my way out," I said. "Would you let Sally across the hall know when you're done? She can lock up and set the alarm for me."

"Sure, thanks. Glad I caught you in. This'll save me a trip."

***

Suzy Lou could not remember the name of the BMW dealership on Billy Mayfair's license plate holder. There were five within 30 miles of San Jose. I cleverly started with the closest one.

I went in the morning, figuring that on a weekday they would not be too busy. I parked my old Prius in a visitor space. As I got out of the car, a smiling salesman appeared as if beamed down. "Can I help you?"

I patted the roof of the Prius. "I think it's time for me to move up, you know what I mean? My friend Billy Mayfair just bought a car here. He said I should talk to his sales person, but I forget the name. We were kinda buzzed at the time…"

The sales guy shook his head. "Mayfair? Name

doesn't ring a bell. I don't think it was me. Let's go find out who helped your friend."

Inside the dealership, I was handed off to the sales manager. After consulting the computer, he told me they had no record of a Mayfair buying a car there in the past year.

"Perhaps he bought it for his company," he said. "That's not unusual here in the Valley."

I scratched my head. "I'm not sure where he's working. You know how engineers hop around. But I do know it was a 6 Series, a red convertible, if that helps."

That indeed helped. The system revealed that there had been only one such car sold by any dealer in the Bay Area in the past month, and it had been delivered by that very dealership, the day before Billy had met Suzy Lou.

By the time he pulled up the details of the sale, I was peering over the sales manager's shoulder. I started memorizing like crazy.

"That was Hector's sale. Today's his day off but..."

I suddenly remembered I had an important meeting in 30 minutes back at the office. I thanked the sales manager, apologized that I had to run, took his card, and promised I'd be back soon to see Hector.

When I got into my car, I pulled out my notebook and wrote down all the details I had memorized about the buyer of the red convertible. A good detective does not rely on his memory for such things. There are too many details that come at you in a case and most are irrelevant. But the one you forget is often crucial. Better to use your brain to think than to remember.

The cool red convertible had been purchased by a Graham Westonovic. Address in Fremont. I also got his DOB and phone number.

I got on the freeway and headed north out of San Jose towards Fremont.

What about my meeting back at the office? Shockingly, I had lied.

Chapter 9

earlier in the year

Stephanie Cunningham was back a week after her first meeting with the Mayfairs. She was right on time, which Sharon appreciated. Sharon was big on punctuality.

Tommy, who referred to Stephanie as the Medicare Lady—he could not recall her name—brightened noticeably when he saw her. Sharon had to admit she was attractive, and Tommy did not get to spend much time with younger women or anyone else aside from her for that matter. She thought it was the attention of a new person more than anything else that pleased him.

After tea was served and some superficial small talk, Stephanie took papers and a pen out of her attaché case. "Today, I'd like to review some basic health care information together. Let's start with medications." She handed them each a sheet of paper. It was the first of what turned out to be a series of checklists they would use over the next several weeks.

Sharon scanned the form. "You can just leave this and we'll go over it later."

Stephanie smiled. She knew that compliance plummeted when clients were left to complete forms on their own. "We've found that it helps if we do it together. Are you in a hurry today?"

Sharon shook her head. "Not really."

"Why not do it now, hon?" Tommy said.

"Oh, all right."

They did four checklists that day. The others were for healthcare providers, tracking appointments, and nutrition and exercise. Later, Sharon admitted to herself that going over the medication checklist had been helpful, especially the part about getting rid of expired or no-longer-used medicine.

Sharon had been suspicious that this was a ploy by Stephanie to take their old meds. She knew all about the opioid crisis and had read about how people sold prescription medication to addicts. But Stephanie did not want the discards. She explained that it would be improper for her to take them. Instead, she helped Sharon bag them and gave her written instructions on where to properly dispose of them.

Stephanie had also supported Sharon when

Final Part

Tommy balked at her advice to schedule some appointments months in advance. That was Sharon's habit; Tommy preferred to procrastinate. "It's better to get them scheduled and then change them if you need to," Stephanie said soothingly. "Good doctors can get booked up. How about we do them now?"

"Why not do it now, Tommy?" Sharon said, smiling indulgently at him. Tommy got on the phone and made the appointments.

After Stephanie left, Sharon started saying "the Medicare Lady said" to get Tommy to do things. It worked well because Tommy did not remember what she had or had not said. But he sure liked the Medicare Lady.

* * *

The checklist for the third visit was about estate planning. As soon as she heard that, Sharon knew what was coming. This was when this lady would start her campaign to become a beneficiary of their estate. It was a standard ploy of in-home caregivers, to curry favor with old folks and get a bequest in their wills.

Sharon was disarmed when Stephanie led off with, "I don't want to know any of the details of what's in your estate plan. That's none of my business. But we'll use this checklist to be sure that you have all the documents you need, they're up-to-date and can be easily accessed when needed."

They had last updated everything three years earlier. The originals were kept at their lawyer's office. Their copies were in a binder that Sharon kept in their home office. By the time Stephanie left, they had agreed that all their documents—living trust, wills, powers-of-attorney, advance directives—were in proper order.

One of the checklist items was to have multiple copies of some of the documents, especially the healthcare powers-of-attorney and advance directives. Stephanie explained that in an emergency, they might have to give copies to more than one provider; best to be prepared.

While Sharon went to get some ibuprofen for Stephanie, who was having some muscle aches that Sharon could readily relate to, Stephanie made the necessary additional copies for them on their home-office printer. When Sharon returned with the pills and a glass of water, she dug out the three-hole-punch and added the new copies behind the appropriate tabs in the binder.

The last item on the checklist was funeral arrangements. It was something that Sharon and Tommy kept postponing. Sharon said she was feeling a bit tired and they needed to stop for the day. Stephanie did not push the issue. She was more than willing to let it slide.

Final Part

* * *

Stephanie Cunningham was glad that the Mayfairs had a fast printer. After she left their home, she stopped at the first parking lot she came to and carefully read the papers she had surreptitiously copied and slipped into her attaché case while Sharon had fetched the ibuprofen. As she read, her smile developed slowly, then burst forth like a flower opening to the sun.

She already had gathered more extensive background on the Mayfairs than what her program provided. She knew all about their estranged son. She was ecstatic to find that, regardless of their animosity, Sharon and Tommy had left everything to their only child, William, and named him their executor.

* * *

Tommy grilled burgers out on the back patio for dinner that evening. He was good at it and Sharon knew Tommy liked feeling competent and helpful. She made corn on the cob—they both still had good teeth—and potato salad.

After dinner, they took their usual seats in the living room. Tommy picked up the remote.

"Before you turn it on," Sharon said, "there's something on my mind."

Tommy knew that was Sharon's way of saying she had something important to discuss and he better pay attention. He put the remote down. "What is it, hon?"

"It's about Billy."

Tommy scowled. Sharon forged on. "I just want to be sure we still want to leave everything to him."

The subject upset Tommy. Billy had lied to them and ripped them off so many times, they had finally severed all ties. Tommy fought the urge to express his feelings about Billy as anger; that would only upset his wife, for no good reason. "We've been over this before. Nothing's changed. We have no one else to leave it to."

"Maybe we could find a charity." The way Sharon said it, it was not a question.

"We went through that exercise, remember?"

Sharon suppressed the urge to point out to Tommy who it was who had trouble remembering things.

"In the end," he went on, "we decided that when we're gone, he gets whatever we have and just maybe it'll help him turn his life around. If not, well, we've done the best we can for our only child."

The conversation had re-opened deep wounds in both their hearts that would never completely heal. Billy had disappointed, then devastated them, time and time again. At least his idiotic decision to move to New York, of all places, had gotten him out of their lives. It had turned out to be a blessing.

Final Part

"At least we won't be here to find out," Sharon said with a sigh.

Tommy reached for the remote.

Chapter 10

I had no idea how this Graham Westonovic and Billy Mayfair were connected, except by the car. But I was detecting. I had a lead. Granted, it was not much of a lead, but you follow the lead you have, not the lead you wish for.

Of course, the clever detective would have done an online search before bucking traffic for a half an hour on a wild-goose chase. I had left my clever at home that morning.

Westonovic's street address turned out to be a postal box at a UPS Store, which I could have learned in no time online. Yet here I was. I went inside. The postal boxes were conveniently located in the front of the store. I looked for Westonovic's unit number. Yes, the box was there. You cannot see inside the boxes, and his refused to speak to me. The lone clerk called to me from behind his counter.

"Can I help you, sir?"

Certain I had wasted my time, I decided to invest a few more minutes and do what detectives mainly do: ask questions in the hope of discovering something

Final Part

useful.

His name was on a tag clipped to his shirt. I decided to use one of my many clever ploys to pry information out of people. I handed Vijay my card. He examined it carefully. "Brink Investigations," he read aloud. "Joe Brink. That is you?"

I nodded, as if he had shrewdly deduced something. "I assume you do not give out information about boxholders."

Vijay looked around, as if someone might overhear us. The place was still empty.

"That is correct, sir. We protect customer confidentiality."

I paused the conversation. If Vijay was open to a bribe, he would soon fill the silence. He did not.

"Good. I'm thinking of getting a box."

Vijay sighed, as if relieved, and his earnest expression added a smile. "I would be most happy to help you."

He proceeded to tell me everything there is to know about renting a postal box, and the associated services they provided, some of which were "a small extra charge." I left with a colorful brochure, and, feeling my clever had returned, the seed of an idea.

Vijay had never asked why someone from Campbell—my office address was on my card—would want a postal box in Fremont. He was not a trained detective.

Phil Bookman

* * *

I drove back to Campbell and did the online research I should have done before traipsing to Fremont. On the way back, I picked up a burrito and a chocolate shake. I needed fuel for my afternoon online.

I was astonished to find that, in the entire United States of America, there was precisely one Graham Westonovic. I was thankful for small favors. He was 35, one of the many wannabee actors on the fringe of the LA entertainment industry. His stage name was Graham West. His biggest part had been on a soap opera about ten years ago, but his character had died of a horrible disease during the first season. Graham had been a busy guy, though, working as an extra on numerous TV shows and movies, some of which even included a sentence of dialog. He had also appeared in quite a few commercials, but rarely with any spoken lines.

Ah, actors. I looked at the many carefully posed images of Graham West online. He was a pleasantly handsome, fit but not muscular looking guy. The kind of man you are sure you have seen before but could not say where. In this case, given all his bit parts and commercials, that would probably be true.

Westonovic/West seemed to be Los Angeles-based, showing several addresses in the region over the years, but I could find none for the last three years. His acting

Final Part

career seemed to have petered out along with the addresses. I called the agency that represented him, posing as a Silicon Valley advertising consultant making a commercial for a tech startup, and was told that Graham West had gone private. When I asked what that meant, I was huffily told to go look it up. Ah, Hollywood!

Look it up I did. Private actors work on a contract basis playing parts for individuals or companies. Want some good-looking folks at your company gala? Need folks to pose as staff members of your startup during a client or potential investor visit? Want someone charming to pose as your partner at your high school reunion? Private actors will handle these and all manner of other parts for short- or long-term engagements. No scripts required. The main skills seem to be improvisation and staying in character.

Some private actors worked for agencies. Others, like Graham, worked freelance and posted their availability on online directories, with each listing linking to the individual's website. But the links to Graham's website were all broken; his site was down.

That was all very interesting, but I still did not know what Westonovic/West had to do with Billy Mayfair.

Chapter 11

earlier in the year

"We have two checklists today," Stephanie said with a big smile. "After that, I'm all out of checklists."

First came the financial checklist. As usual, Stephanie seemed to anticipate Sharon's wariness. "I don't want the details of your finances. That's none of my business. But we've found that financial problems are one of the biggest contributors to poor health."

"We own our home," Tommy said, his voice tinged with pride. "Paid it off years ago. Same for the car. We are debt free."

"That's great! What about credit card debt?"

"We pay everything off monthly, right Sharon?"

"Always. I pay the bills now," Sharon said. She took Tommy's hand. "Tommy used to manage our finances, but he started having a problem with details."

It wasn't the first time Tommy's failing memory

Final Part

had come up during their meetings. Stephanie noted that neither of them seemed to have a problem when it did. It was simply a fact of life.

"How about income?" Stephanie asked a series of questions. Tommy received social security, Sharon, a public employee's pension. They had about a million dollars in savings in Tommy's IRA that had come from his 401-k, and took the minimum required annual distributions. Stephanie never asked for specific income or savings amounts; they just seemed to slip out from her clients.

"We have no problem paying our bills," Sharon said, after they answered the items on the expenses section of the checklist.

Stephanie agreed. The Mayfairs were in excellent financial shape. They lived modestly, well within their income. She did not comment on the millions of dollars of equity the Mayfairs had in their home. She did a mental calculation and figured their net worth was about five million dollars, but they did not live like millionaires. She had seen this before with her elderly clients. The value of their homes often did not figure in their sense of their net worth.

The last checklist was about social support systems. Medicare's social isolation index was calculated from data gleaned from medical records. Medicare increasingly required healthcare providers to gather a variety of kinds of information from patients that traditionally had not been captured by medical professionals, some of which were specifically for the SII calculation. The Mayfairs had been selected by computer for the program based on their SII. Usually, this checklist was done at the first meeting, to double-check the SII and confirm eligibility. But Stephanie had flexibility in that. The Mayfairs were special to her, and she had chosen to do it last.

It did not take long to complete. The Mayfairs had come from Pennsylvania. Most of their relatives were still there or in Florida or South Carolina. Other than Christmas cards, they had little contact with them.

Their only child, William, was a sore point. "He's in New York," Sharon said. "We don't communicate." Tommy looked away. Subject closed. Which was fine with Stephanie.

The Mayfairs did not belong to a church or any other group, together or individually. They often went to lectures at Stanford, usually about science, and went to a classical music concert about once a quarter. Otherwise, they were homebodies.

As for friends, Tommy had an old army buddy he had lunch with about once a month, and the three of them got together for a barbecue a couple of times a year. Sharon admitted to being friendly with her housekeeper, who came once a week, and the woman who did her hair. But no, no intimate friends.

Final Part

Stephanie wanted to be certain on this point. Pointing to the 50th wedding anniversary photo, Stephanie said, "Was that taken at your party?"

The Mayfairs exchanged puzzled looks. "No party. That was taken at our anniversary dinner by the maître d' at the French place," Tommy said. "We go there every year for our anniversary."

"Le Papillon," Sharon reminded him.

Le Papillon was an elegant, upscale French restaurant, a fine place for an anniversary dinner. "Who else was there with you?"

Sharon reached for Tommy's hand and smiled lovingly. "Just the two of us."

They're certainly isolated, *Stephanie thought.* But not lonely. They have each other.

* * *

Stephanie changed the schedule from weekly meetings to every other week. Later, she explained, they would go to monthly. They had worked through all the checklists, and she told the Mayfairs that her future visits would be mainly to check in with them and be sure they were doing okay. They could, of course, call her anytime.

After Stephanie Cunningham left, Tommy said he was disappointed at the change in schedule. Sharon was surprised to find that she shared that view, though she kept it to herself.

As she drove away, Stephanie Cunningham uncharacteristically whooped for joy and punched the air. Then she called her cousin.

Chapter 12

I had just completed an insurance fraud case. This time the purportedly fully disabled bozo had spent the weekend water skiing with friends, using his own boat, on Clear Lake, about three hours north of Silicon Valley.

Mr. Bozo lived in the sort of middle-income residential neighborhood of single family homes where it's difficult to stake out a house. A parked car with someone sitting inside stands out and you can expect to be noticed and challenged. Instead, I had a friend, Ricky Clancy, who drove for Uber, drive past Mr. Bozo's house several times a day. Ricky noticed him spending most of Friday packing gear into the boat in his driveway, then hitching it to the back of his SUV.

Paying work trumps *pro bono*, so that night, I attached a GPS device to the underside of the SUV. Next morning, Anna and I took a leisurely drive to Clear Lake, followed the GPS signal at a comfortable distance, and I took about a hundred photos and an hour of video of the moron cavorting with his family on his water skis.

Anna and I spent that night and the next day enjoying the lake, courtesy of the insurance company. I knew they would gladly pay my travel expenses, along with my usual fee, including what I paid Ricky, for such quick work catching Bozo displaying his robust good health.

Which gave me an idea. The police may not have been interested in investigating the Mayfair deaths, but I had an idea who would. Maybe I could turn this into a paying case after all.

First thing Monday morning, I emailed the incriminating files to my boss at the insurance company, then immediately called and told him the good news about Mr. Bozo. Duly softened up, he was more than willing to do me the small favor I requested. While it wasn't his company, he tapped into a database that revealed the Mayfairs' auto insurance carrier. I called them and eventually talked to the gal handling the claim Billy Mayfair had filed.

I told Indira Kapoor who I was, used my insurance company boss as a reference, and said that, in the course of another investigation, I had come across information that gave me reason to believe the Mayfairs had not died accidentally.

"Would you be interested in contracting with me to investigate the Mayfair accident?"

"Can I put you on hold a minute?"

Final Part

Before I could answer, I was listening to canned music.

I was patient in the pursuit of paying work. It took about five minutes for Indira to come back on the line; it seemed like 20.

"Mr. Brink, I think we can work something out."

Music to my ears.

It was not the claim on the vehicle that had excited Indira Kapoor. The car wasn't worth that much. But Tommy Mayfair had a $250,000 accidental death and dismemberment policy, and both of the Mayfairs had $250,000 term life policies. If it had not been an accident, they could at a minimum refuse to pay on the ADD policy. Depending on what had actually happened, the other policies could also come into play. Nothing motivates an insurance company quite like the prospect of avoiding paying a big claim.

Chapter 13

Allie Chen had been born in China. When they arrived in California, her parents had changed her name to Alabaster, the English translation of her Chinese name, a name much favored in their home region.

Allie was a freelance forensic artist. She worked with smaller law enforcement departments that could not afford their own sketch artists—that was what they were called, even though these days they did their work on an iPad using a special app—as well as private investigators and anyone else willing to pay her hourly rate. Which I was, courtesy of Indira Kapoor and the insurance company she worked for.

I knew Allie would have worked for me for free, but I did not want to take advantage of that. It came about when Allie's younger brother, George, was mistakenly arrested for armed robbery in a small Arizona town near Tucson, where he attended the University of Arizona. It was a case of "all young Chinese guys look alike" to the all-white desert town police force.

It took me a day to prove his alibi. At the time of the holdup, George had been 30 miles away, at a concert

Final Part

on campus, and I not only found witnesses, I got security camera video to back their statements. George's mistake was to go for a drive in the desert the next day and stop for a beer in the wrong little town.

George had been the reason the Chen's left China. It was during the era of the one-child policy, and when Mrs. Chen became pregnant for the second time, they began the arduous, dangerous, illegal journey that brought them to California. Though they had paid me for my work, the family now believed they owed me a lifetime debt which, Allie told me, could not be cancelled.

* * *

It was always easier to look for someone when you had a picture to show people. I needed a picture of Billy Mayfair. I could find none online. He had dropped out of high school at 16, so was not in a yearbook. Boomer was pretty sure he had not been around locally for years before his parents' deaths, and I did not want to take the time or expense of going to New York to see what I could dig up.

I called Suzy Lou. She said she thought it would be fun to work with Allie to create a likeness of Billy. But Suzy was in Hawaii for the week, a gift she had given herself from the commission on the Mayfair home sale. She assured me that she would get together with Allie after she returned from her tropical getaway.

*** * * ***

I would be getting a nice payment from the water-skiing-bozo insurance case. Best Buy was offering a great deal on a 65-inch TV with free delivery. It was serendipity, and I placed the order online and Sally volunteered to wait for delivery at my place on her afternoon off. Thank you, Mr. Bozo.

I had already run an Ethernet cable to the living room. It was much faster than Wi-Fi and would give me smooth, instant streaming. The cable box was installed. All we had to do was mount the set on the wall and hook it up.

That evening, after Sally and Anna agreed on the perfect position for the monster TV, I installed the mounting bracket on the wall. With three of us, we had an easy time getting the TV mounted.

The last step was positioning the speakers I had brought from my bedroom at home to surround us with sound. Now I had my own home theater.

I turned the TV on and did a bit of setup using the remotes, one for the TV, one for the cable box. Then I programmed the cable remote to operate the TV, so I didn't need to use two of them.

Anna went down the hall and invited Jonathan and Charles over. The guys brought two bottles of red wine.

Final Part

We ordered in pizza from MySlice and were soon arguing over what movie to watch.

Chapter 14

earlier in the year

On a cold, gray New York day, Billy Mayfair walked away from the South Bronx residential drug diversion program that had gotten him early release from Rikers Island. He was bouncing a little, getting his walk going, though it was hard to be cool wearing a backpack over a hoodie.

Billy had completed the program and was a free man again. He'd already had his last appointment with his PO, and, as long as he could find a place to live and keep a job for a while, he was home free. That, and avoiding the cops. He wanted to stay out of jail, sure, that was why he had followed the rules, been a good boy, and stuck with the program. But Billy did not do well with "free." Absent imposed, rigid structure, he had a hard time connecting his actions to consequences. Yet the consequences kept coming.

Final Part

But Billy was not a deep thinker, certainly not a self-aware one. He had difficulty connecting cause and effect, especially when he was the cause and an arrest was the effect.

Right now, Billy Mayfair's priorities were clear: Get some cash, get high, get laid.

Get dead was not on the list.

* * *

Dude came up behind him, almost like he'd been waiting for Billy. Probably waiting for someone like me, *Billy thought. A man with an itch to scratch, a customer.*

On the streets, you were either predator or prey. Billy was a predator. Not a very good one, but streetwise enough to survive, if sometimes just barely. His lizard brain twitched. Dude was sizing him up. Maybe as a buyer of whatever he had to sell, or maybe as prey. Billy was on high alert.

Dude walked right next to Billy, like they were just two homies strolling along. Dude said, "You look like a man with a need."

"Got that right, bro. Thing is, I'm sort of broke."

Dude said, "Maybe I can help with both problems."

Dude did not sound like he was from these streets, but Billy, caution giving way to appetite, was not willing to pass up an opportunity. They walked in silence for another block. Dude turned into an alley, stopped by an RV.

Dude said, "My ride. You in?"
Billy Mayfair was in.

Chapter 15

Boomer and I were enjoying burgers at Greasy Jack's. He ordered fries, I ordered onion rings, and we shared. The place was packed as usual at lunchtime and the acoustics were awful, which made it a great place to have a private conversation.

I had updated Boomer on my progress on the case, including my online research. He was unimpressed.

"Bottom line, you went to Fremont to find this Westonovic guy and struck out."

"It accomplished one useful thing."

"What might that be?"

"It got me thinking about Fremont."

"Other than being the last stop for BART, what's there to think about?"

"Exactly!" When I was a teenager, during the summer we would hitch a ride to the Bay Area Rapid Transit station in Fremont and take the train into the city to San Francisco Giants and Oakland A's games. Otherwise, as far as I knew, there was no there there. "So why would a slick Hollywood dude like Westonovic live in Fremont, of all places? And, if he did, why go all the way to San Jose to buy a car? There's a BMW dealer right there."

"I bet you're about to reveal the answer," Boomer said, as I swooped in for fries. He was snatching onion rings off my plate faster than I was snagging fries from his, and I was determined to catch up.

I chewed my mouthful of fries, letting the suspense build. "It's the old postal box misdirection ploy."

Boomer laughed so hard he almost choked. "What the hell is that?"

"You take out a postal box someplace far from where you live, but not at the post office, at one of the private postal service places. Then go to the post office that serves the place and put in a change of address form. The mail never goes to the postal box, but senders don't know that, they think it's your address."

"You think Westonovic did that?"

"I know it."

"How?"

"After I left the UPS Store, I went to the post office nearby. I addressed an envelope to Westonovic's postal box and mailed it with 'do not forward' instructions. It came back yesterday, returned to sender because of those instructions."

Boomer looked at me with a squint and a grin. "Nice work, detective."

"I still don't know why. And I don't know where he is. But it sure is suspicious."

Final Part

As Boomer snatched the last onion ring, he said, "What the hell are Billy Mayfair and Graham Westonovic up to?"

We decided to get chocolate shakes for a mental energy boost. When we returned to our table, I said, "The one thing we have going for us is that they have no idea anyone is looking for them."

"Actually, they don't know *we're* looking for them. That box forwarding thing tells me Westonovic is hiding from someone."

Boomer was right. That could work to our advantage. I just had no idea how.

* * *

Back in the office, I got to thinking about there being just one Graham Westonovic in the country. Out of over 300 million people, that was remarkable. I wondered how many there were with the last name of Westonovic. I looked it up. According to 2010 census data, there were 47. It was not a popular surname.

I then logged into a database that claims to have the name and address of nearly every adult in the United States. They use algorithms to remove duplicate people, that is, they merge address and phone number data for the same person, creating a historical view. It's where I had found Graham's addresses in the Los Angeles area, but nothing for the last few years, not even a listed phone number.

Bottom line, I found 18 Westonovic households with current phone numbers. I started calling.

People don't answer their phones that much anymore. Many let most calls go to voicemail, especially when they don't recognize the caller ID. So, when I left a message, I had to make my pitch good.

I said I was an old buddy of Graham's, hadn't seen him in a few years, and wanted to let him know that a mutual friend had passed away. Were they related? Did they know how to reach him?

I had set up a phone number account with an online service—no actual phone line, it all happened in the cloud. The recorded message said, "Hi, I'm not available now. Please leave a message." No name, nothing about Brink Investigations. I used that phone number when I wanted to be anonymous or, like now, incognito.

Calling myself Cole Spenser, I worked my way through the list, leaving messages. I reached a real person on the fifth call. The detective gods were smiling on me. She was Graham's Aunt Hilda from Indianapolis. Hadn't seen the lad in years, since he went to Hollywood to become a star but, sadly, did not. She thought her daughter might know how to reach him; she and her cousin had stayed in touch.

Aunt Hilda refused to give me her daughter's name or number. It was the prudent thing to do, and I didn't

Final Part

push it. "I'll give Stevie your name and number, and she can decide," she said.

Oops. I smiled and thanked Aunt Hilda.

I continued my way through the listings. I reached three more people, none of whom would give me the time of day. I never got any callbacks from the messages I left. The Westonovics were keen on privacy.

Chapter 16

earlier in the year

Late in the afternoon, on a fine spring day, Stephanie Cunningham knocked on the Mayfairs' front door. It was her last appointment for the day.

Sharon greeted her pleasantly. "What's in the box?" You could not see the street through the trees, so Sharon did not notice that Stephanie's car wasn't there; she had been dropped off by an Uber driver.

Stephanie handed the white box with its pretty red bow to Sharon. "These are for you."

They took their seats in the living room and Sharon opened the box. "Look, Tommy, brownies!"

"I made them myself last night." Stephanie knew they were a favorite of both her clients, intelligence gathered from completing a nutrition checklist at an earlier visit.

Sharon served tea, but Tommy had a glass of milk

Final Part

instead. Stephanie explained that she was allergic to chocolate but wanted Sharon and Tommy to enjoy the treat.

"It would be impolite not to," Tommy said. Even Sharon laughed.

* * *

An hour later, Sharon and Tommy were unconscious. They would stay that way for at least eight hours. Stephanie needed about six.

Stephanie left them sleeping in their chairs. Time to clean up. She rinsed the teapot, cups, saucers, plates and spoons, and put them in the dishwasher, added detergent and started it. She removed every trace of the brownies, putting the leftovers and crumbs back in the box, then slid the ribbon and bow back on.

Now for the hard part. Stephanie donned gloves, not to disguise that she had been there, but rather, where she had been besides in the living room and kitchen.

Stephanie took the car keys out of Sharon's purse, went out the back door and around into the carport from the rear. She unlocked the car, opened both front doors, and put the front seat all the way back. The carport opened to the side, so this activity was hidden from the street.

Sharon weighed barely 100 pounds. Stephanie put

plastic bags over her feet and shoes and tied them in place, then dragged the woman out the back door, to the front passenger side of the car, maneuvered her into the seat, belted her in, removed the plastic bags, and closed the door.

Stephanie silently thanked the heavens that the Mayfairs owned an old Chevy Impala that had a bench front seat. If the car had bucket seats, this plan would not have worked, and she would have had to come up with something else that she could pull off on her own.

She repeated the process with Tommy, but he was much heavier than his wife. Stephanie reminded herself to be methodical, that she had plenty of time. She rolled Tommy onto a throw rug, gripped the rug with both hands and, walking backwards, dragged him from the living room to the driver's side of the car. Struggling, she leaned him inside behind the steering wheel, legs still outside the car. She took a break, gathered her strength and maneuvered Tommy into the center of the front seat. Getting Sharon belted in had been a cinch; doing so for Tommy, not so easy. But she got it done.

Then she put the rug back in its place and waited until midnight.

* * *

Final Part

Gloves back on, Stephanie squeezed herself in next to Tommy, behind the steering wheel, drove out of the maze of narrow streets to Los Gatos-Saratoga Road and turned right. She dropped the box of brownies in a dumpster at a diner as she entered Los Gatos. Moments later, she turned onto 17 and began the climb up into the Santa Cruz Mountains. But not for long. She soon turned left off 17 onto Alma Bridge Road and slowly made her way around to the east side of Lexington Reservoir.

Stephanie came to a sharp bend in the road and easily found the spot she wanted; she had scouted it several times, twice at night to be sure she wouldn't miss the opening in the trees that lined the manmade lake.

She pulled onto, then over, the shoulder, put the car in park, opened the front windows a crack, set the brake and got out. She moved Tommy to the driver's seat, put the keys in his pocket, positioned him just so and belted him in.

Stephanie took a deep breath, reached inside through the open door, released the parking brake, shifted into drive and watched as the car crept along, then gathered speed as it reached the steep incline that took it into the water. The splash seemed deafening to her, but there was no one else to hear it.

She uncovered the motor scooter hidden in the tangle of brush where she had left it earlier. Stephanie puttered off, back the way she came. From the time she had left the freeway in the Mayfairs' car until she drove back onto it riding the scooter, she had not seen another person or vehicle.

Chapter 17

The Law Offices of Wardell Chamberlin Esq. were on the third floor of an aging building located a few blocks from the courthouse in downtown San Jose. The whole shabby area was being redeveloped. Dell's forlorn building was surrounded by temporary parking lots which had sprung up when the buildings that had been there were torn down. They were interspersed with huge rusted dumpsters and random piles of rubble. Dell's practice was housed in what looked like the lone surviving structure after an apocalypse. It, too, would soon see the wrecking ball.

I was there to get my first case assignment. Dell's secretary showed me right into his office. Dell's furnishings and accommodations were no better than my own. My face must have shown my surprise.

"We'll be moving in about a year," he said. "Into a new tower going up out there." He gestured in the direction of the dusty window, with its dismal view of cars and crap. At least I got funky, lively Campbell Avenue.

The secretary brought Dell coffee and me a soda.

Then he told me about the Conrad case.

Timothy Conrad was single, the divorced, middle-aged owner of a small general contracting company. He lived alone and made a decent living but was by no means wealthy. He had nothing more serious on his record than a few traffic tickets. Tim was out on bail, charged with manslaughter in the death of Ruby Swanson.

"Tim was drinking in a bar on a Friday night, "Dell said. "He picked up Ruby Swanson, a woman he had never met before. The two left together sometime around 11 p.m. Maybe ten minutes later, another couple were heading for their car and came across Ruby Swanson's body in the parking lot, next to her car. The guy called 9-1-1. Paramedics and cops arrived. Ruby was DOA. Her head had been bashed in, probably with a large crescent wrench. The cops have witnesses who place the couple together in the bar. The cocktail waitress who settled their bill remembers them being in a hurry to leave, and Tim's credit card receipt confirms the time."

Dell leaned back in his chair. "So, tell me what you think so far."

"Guy picks up a woman in a bar. They drink awhile, leave together in a rush, maybe head for his car. He's a contractor, so it's probably a truck. He wants sex, maybe thinks she's already agreed. She declines, they argue, she heads for her car, he grabs a wrench out of

Final Part

his truck, goes after her, maybe they argue some more, and he kills her in a drunken rage."

Dell nodded. "Yet they almost didn't charge him. Why?"

I thought a bit. "It's all circumstantial. I bet there's no physical evidence. They never found the wrench with her blood on it and her blood wasn't on Tim or his clothes or vehicle. They had no witness to them arguing or the altercation." Altercation was one of the A words from the vocabulary builder app I had recently put on my phone.

Dell smiled. "Very good. Yet now our client is awaiting trial for manslaughter."

"Did he confess?"

"Nope."

"They later found physical evidence?"

"Nope."

"Then they must have found a witness," I said.

"Bingo!"

"What's our client say?" Our, not your. I was done with tryouts. I'd played Dell's little game and had either made the team or I was out of there.

"He says it was his first time at that bar; he was trying a new place. He had just met Ruby, also for the first time. They drank and talked and hit it off. The time got away from them. She had to relieve her sitter by 11:30. He wanted to get a good night's sleep because it was his weekend with the kids. So he paid the check, walked her to her car. They exchanged phone numbers; their cell phones confirm that. They also shared a goodnight kiss. She got in the car and he headed for his truck and drove home. Tim says he never actually saw her drive away."

"I assume my job is to discredit the witness," I said.

"That, or find evidence pointing to someone else. It doesn't have to be airtight, or even be the real killer, though that would be preferable. I just need enough to create reasonable doubt."

Dell gave me everything he had on the witness and victim. It wasn't much, but, then, that's usually how a case starts.

As I was leaving, he said, "You do have the kind of time this case needs, don't you?"

"Of course. I understand what's at stake for our client."

"It's just that I was wondering if that insurance case was taking up a lot of your time, you know, the Mayfield case."

"It's Mayfair. And don't worry, you can count on me."

As I drove back to my office, I felt the weight of my new responsibility. If I could not discredit the witness who claimed she saw Tim Conrad and Ruby Swanson in a heated argument, moments before her death, or find another good suspect, he was looking at years in prison.

Final Part

This was the kind of juicy case I wanted when I became a PI. But at the time, all I could think of was, "Be careful what you wish for."

Chapter 18

earlier in the year

As he walked along the sidewalk mumbling to himself, with scraggily long hair and beard, unkempt clothes, and just a little wild-eyed, Billy Mayfair went unnoticed. In most places, he would have stood out, been someone you would give a wide berth, maybe even cross the street to avoid. Not here. In this dingy but crowded section of Queens, Billy was just another piece of unpleasant human flotsam heading for work amidst an anonymous, uncaring throng of the studiously oblivious.

"I'm a 30-year-old fuckup. Been clean for a few months. Holding on by a thread. Gotta just focus on keeping my job, staying clean and out of trouble."

It was the mantra he had repeated countless times since he left drug diversion. He mumbled it aloud. No one paid attention.

Final Part

Arriving at the steel door next to the loading dock in the rear of the shabby old building, Billy clocked in and began his workday. For eight and a half hours, less a half hour for lunch, he would move stuff from the racks in the vast warehouse to the loading dock, then move other crap from the loading dock to the racks. It was like digging holes and filling them up; work for prisoners in a cartoon.

Billy was one of the few guys in the place who spoke only English. Spanish and several Eastern European languages prevailed. This, along with his "I'm a bit off" vibe, made it easy for Billy to avoid most conversation with his coworkers. He showed up on time, did his work, got lunch from a roach coach, worked some more, went home to his tenement. Repeat.

The call came in on his cheap pay-as-you-go phone just before lunchtime. Billy did not recognize the number, but then again, he hardly ever got a call.

Five minutes later, Billy told his boss he would have to leave early.

"Got a call from a cop in California. My parents are dead. Some kind of car accident. I gotta go home."

"Finish your shift," his boss said. "You can't help them now." The boss was skeptical. He heard all manner of excuses for missing work from his less than reliable staff. But even if the guy was telling him the truth, he didn't imagine Billy could have ever been a help to his parents or anyone else for that matter. He

decided to be kind and keep that to himself.

"Nope," Billy said. "Leaving now. And won't be back."

No longer feeling kind, the boss issued an imaginative string of profanity. Billy did not care.

* * *

Billy's belongings, including his laptop, fit into his backpack. He rented the hovel month-to-month, no lease, no deposit. Also no Wi-Fi, but he had been able to piggyback onto the guest network of someone's nearby cable gateway. Billy put the room key in an envelope, wrote a brief note on the outside, and slipped it under the super's door.

In the taxi to JFK, Billy recited to himself: "I'm a 30-year-old fuckup. Been clean for a few months. Holding on by a thread. Gotta go home now and handle my dead parents' affairs."

It was Billy Mayfair's new, improved mantra.

Chapter 19

Downtown Campbell consisted of a few blocks along Campbell Avenue packed with eateries and foot traffic. The folks at the bakery and the yogurt shop on the ground floor of our building would seize on any excuse to throw a party. They said it pulled people in off the sidewalk and was good for business. Free donuts and fro-yo for a couple of hours worked for me. Our cost for the party Sally and I organized for Mr. Vu was zero.

Mr. Vu had been bewildered when I told him we were giving him a retirement party but warmed up to the idea after Sally explained it to him. His only request was that we not invite his clients, friends or family. They would have their own celebration in their own manner, he said.

However, Mr. Vu brought his long-time business partner, Mr. Chu to the festivities. Mr. Chu had developed Alzheimer's a while back and now lived in a nearby memory care facility. Mr. Vu was Mr. Chu's conservator. I believed that Mr. Chu's situation had prompted Mr. Vu to take stock of his life and accelerate his retirement plans.

Mr. Chu no longer knew who any of us were—he even seemed a bit vague about Mr. Vu. But, on the plus side, Mr. Chu was no longer shy and reserved; he was full of smiles and laughter, and joined in the partying with gusto, especially the fro-yo and donuts. Mr. Vu was paying an aide from the care facility to keep an eye on Mr. Chu and be sure he was safe and didn't wander.

Signs announcing the retirement party were put out on the sidewalk at 7 p.m. It was a balmy evening and downtown Campbell was alive with folks strolling along, many of whom were looking for a place to eat, drink or grab a snack. By 7:15, the bakery and fro-yo shop were packed with miscellaneous well-wishers, overflowing out onto the wide sidewalk where tables and chairs invited hanging out. Few of the partygoers had any idea who Mr. Vu was. This did not seem to faze either him or them.

* * *

Anna and I were out on the sidewalk, arguing about the top-ten list for types of donuts—we agreed on only five of the ten— when Dell Chamberlin came up to us. When I met with him earlier in the day, I had invited him to the party. And the party was a nice way for me to forget about the burden of the Conrad case, if only temporarily.

"Nice party, Joe," Dell said, smiling at Anna, not me.

Final Part

I introduced them to each other.

I spotted Boomer across the room. Not one to pass up free donuts, he was chatting animatedly with Mr. Chu. I left Anna talking to Dell, who was semi-hitting on her, which I could see pleased and amused her.

As I approached, Boomer broke away from Chu, and we walked out of the bakery and into the fro-yo shop for a change of pace. We eyeballed the offerings. "You and Mr. Chu seemed to be into it," I said.

"We were both fighting on the same side in Nam. Funny thing is, Hung remembers it as if it happened yesterday. I'm going to talk to Vu and get on Hung's visitor's list, drop in for a chat every once in a while."

That made me feel good. I knew Mr. Chu's first name was Hung. It had been on their office door in big letters. I'd just never heard anyone call him by it before.

Dell appeared on the other side of me, apparently intrigued by the many fro-yo offerings. I introduced him to Boomer, then we resumed our conversation while Dell tasted a few flavors.

I told Boomer about the progress I had made on my Westonovic hunt and that I was waiting for Graham's cousin to call me. Boomer shook his head and eyed me skeptically. "What are the odds of that happening? Sounds like a hope and a prayer."

"Ah, but this trained detective does not rely on hopes and prayers. I also turned up a lead."

"What might that be?"

"Graham's Aunt Hilda let slip that this cousin, her daughter, is named Stevie."

Boomer shook his head in dismay. "What the hell kind of a name is that for a girl?"

"It's a nickname for Stephanie. I think Stevie Nicks made it popular." In truth, until I had googled "what girl's name is Stevie a nickname for" I had never heard of Stevie Nicks. Before my time.

Boomer grinned. "Fleetwood Mac. My generation's music."

"My lead," I said.

"You guys got any frozen yogurt favorites to recommend?" Dell asked.

I had forgotten he was there.

Chapter 20

Suzy Lou was enjoying her unexpected getaway to Maui. It was just after spring break and she had managed to get a decent room at a Kaanapali resort on short notice.

She was still connected to her job by phone. Her office messages were forwarded to her cell phone. Suzy had no active listings, just a couple of house-hunting clients. She was an old pro in the business and would be able to keep them at bay for a week. Meanwhile, Suzy was committed to working on her tan and sampling a wide variety of fruity rum drinks.

Suzy was at the pool bar, where the bartender suggested she try a dark rum Piña Colada. She readily agreed.

While she was watching her drink being prepared, a woman about her age took the seat next to her. Unlike Suzy, who was in her black bikini, the woman's beachwear was a white coverup and white shorts, topped off with a floppy white hat.

The bartender placed Suzy's drink, garnished with a cherry and slice of pineapple, on a cardboard coaster.

"Let me know what you think," he said. Then, to the other woman, "Aloha. What can I get you?"

"I'll try what she's having. Looks good."

Twenty minutes later, Suzy and her new friend had agreed to meet for dinner.

* * *

A few miles north of the old fishing village of Lahaina, Route 30 climbs up the west side of Maui, past the beach resort towns of Kaanapali, Napili and Kapalua. Then, leaving sandy beaches and most traces of civilization behind, it narrows to barely two lanes, hugging the coast, winding and climbing along rugged cliffs with breathtaking views of the ocean and the neighboring island of Molokai, accompanied by towering drop-offs to the rock-strewn shoreline.

There are few places along this treacherous stretch with enough shoulder for a car to pull off the road, fewer still with enough straightaway to safely turn around. However spectacular the views, the driver needs to remain patient and alert, focused on the road ahead.

* * *

Near the north tip of Maui, the white car stood out against the black, volcanic gravel beach. It had bounced

Final Part

off several rock ledges on its way down. A passerby the next day spotted it and reported it to 9-1-1. Responders had quite a time making their way down to where the wreck lay, about 50 feet below the road.

They found Suzy Lou's broken body several yards from the shore, floating in an eddy pool the ocean had carved over eons in a huge boulder.

* * *

Stephanie tried to sleep on the flight home, but intrusive thoughts would not let her drop off.

She had no idea what Graham had been thinking. It was bad enough he had bought that flashy, attention-getting car so soon. Worse, he had driven it to the realtor's, taken a photo of Suzy Lou in front of her office admiring it, then inexplicably texted it to Stephanie as if that proved he was following the plan. If the realtor had happened to look at the temporary registration on the windshield, she would have seen the name was not William Mayfair.

But that alone wasn't what had prompted Stephanie to action. Aunt Hilda had called and told her some guy with a 408 area code was trying to contact cousin Graham. What were the chances that this so-called old buddy would just happen to be from Silicon Valley? Slim to none. Someone was after Graham for something. Had he made someone suspicious about their little project? Like, maybe, this Suzy Lou? Stephanie was not taking any chances. She needed to clean up after Graham. Pronto.

She had admonished her flakey cousin using their agreed mode of communication: text messages over burner phones. He had become paranoid about phone calls, convinced that the NSA and who knew who else were listening in; instead, they used a messaging app where the messages disappeared.

Graham texted back that he had let his exuberance get the best of him and promised to behave. He was just feeling giddy at how well their plan was working.

Stephanie had also pressed him to wire her share of the money he had gotten from the Mayfair accounts into the account she had set up for that purpose. He had put her off, saying it would take a few more days to get most of the money because it was in an online brokerage account and he'd had to mail them the necessary paperwork after he'd gotten a form notarized. That had gone fine, Graham said; he had Billy's New York driver's license, had learned how to smoothly forge his signature, and the notary had barely glanced at it anyway. Graham was using makeup and hair color to approximate Billy's appearance in his driver's license photo, and he fooled the notary just as he had the TSA agent when he had flown in from New York. He had bought the car with the cash from the Mayfairs' local

Final Part

bank savings and checking accounts, which had a combined total of about $80,000. Lots less, now that he'd bought the car.

Stephanie trusted cousin Graham. They had been close their entire lives, shared secrets, had each other's back. They had navigated the treacherous waters of the Westonovic family together. She told herself not to be impatient when the end was so near, not to quibble over a few thousand dollars given what was at stake. The closing on the property sale was just a few days off. Then both she and her cousin would each be two-and-a-half million dollars richer. And sooner or later, they would split the proceeds of the Mayfairs' insurance policies, a sort of cherry on the sundae.

* * *

Suzy Lou had been easy to find. Stephanie had called and reached her on her cell phone, pretending to be a new client who simply had to work with Suzy. She laughed with Suzy when told she had reached her on the beach in Maui. Suzy, ever the salesperson, worked on bonding with her new client. By the time the call ended, they had made an appointment for when Suzy returned home the following week. And Stephanie knew the resort where Suzy was staying. Stephanie booked the next available seat on a flight to Maui.

Suzy never connected the voice on the phone with

the friendly lady she met at the bar, who called herself Hope. And Stephanie was careful not to communicate further with Suzy by phone, which could have left a trail back to her.

Suzy was happy to drive them to the old outdoor restaurant, where they ordered from a little shack, sat at an aging picnic table, ate fish tacos and drank Mai Tais poured from a pitcher. More accurately, Suzy drank Mai Tais. Her friend Hope volunteered to stick to fizzy water and drive them back. Suzy thought that was a fine, generous thing to do.

After dinner, Suzy fell into a drunken stupor as soon as the car started moving. Stephanie was thankful for the full moon and cloudless sky, without which she doubted she could have found the isolated location she had selected earlier. She encountered no cars in either direction once they got north of Kapalua.

Once at the right spot, Stephanie easily transferred her sleeping victim into the driver's seat, wiped the car for prints—she had been careful where she touched—and rolled it over the cliff. Then she located the rented moped she had stashed out of sight on the side of the road. She had loaded it in the back of her rented SUV, driven out and put it in position that afternoon.

Stephanie wondered if rolling cars off deserted roads and over drop-offs into bodies of water and stashing a scooter as a getaway vehicle was becoming her MO. She had never imagined she would ever even

Final Part

have an MO. But that was before Vern had transformed into the Bastard.

Ah, well, time to head back to the mainland and deal with whoever this Cole Spenser was who was looking for Graham.

Chapter 21

Widow O'Toole's was a neighborhood bar on a busy street in a middle-class suburban San Jose neighborhood, next to but not in a strip mall that was anchored by Dominici's, an independent supermarket. The parking lots were not connected; you had to drive out onto the street to get from the bar's lot to the mall's.

The bar itself had been there for over 50 years, under several different names and owners. The current owner had bought the place after her husband died of a heart attack, thus the name.

I got there at about 9:30 p.m. and went inside. The place had a semi-Irish flavor, as if the widow had only tried half-heartedly to cash in on her husband's heritage. There was a lot of green glass, including the lampshades, and shamrocks on the wall along with the requisite leprechaun logo, but otherwise it was your typical suburban, almost-but-not-quite-yuppie bar. It was well-lit and clean, and the floor and furniture were in decent condition and not sticky. Even the restrooms were tidy and smelled okay.

The long bar, lined with oak wood stools, ran along

one wall. A dozen or so shiny oak tables with matching chairs filled the middle area, and oak booths with dark green upholstery ran down the other wall. There was the requisite dart board behind the seating area, and a hall in the back that led to the usual collection of restrooms, closets and offices. At the end of the bar was a pass-through window to a small kitchen.

There was no dance floor, pool table or jukebox. There were no TVs showing miscellaneous athletic events. There was no annoying, intrusive background music. This was a place for adults to drink, maybe grab a bite, and chat with friends.

I didn't think it would attract many habitual solitary drinkers, and I couldn't spot any at the bar. I wanted to get a feel for the place, so I had a burger and a beer at the bar. I'm not much of a beer drinker but I wanted to blend in. I told the bartender I was waiting for a friend.

It was a weeknight and the place was about half full of folks you might otherwise see at any of the shops in the mall next door. It was noisy, but it was the noise of happy chatter among friends. I was there about a half-hour and noticed nothing noteworthy, meaning nothing I thought might help our case.

Other than ordering, I left without talking to anyone. But I liked the place. It had an unpretentious, upbeat vibe. They made a decent cheeseburger. I thought I might bring Anna there sometime.

Phil Bookman

* * *

The lighting in Widow O'Toole's blacktop parking lot was not very good but was adequate for its purpose. I knew exactly where Ruby Swanson had been parked. One of the light poles was at the head of the well-marked space, and the light was working. I made a note to check if it had been working on the night she had died.

The bar lot was separated from the mall by a cinderblock wall. The mall lot sloped up from the street, whereas the bar lot was level. The result was that the mall stores were about two feet higher than the bar. Ruby had been parked head-in to the wall. The wall on the bar side was five feet high, but on the mall side at that point it was about three feet high.

I stood on the mall side looking down at Ruby Swanson's parking space. That was where the witness said she had parked and seen Ruby and Tim arguing. If so, she would have had an excellent view of any activity around Ruby's car.

Chapter 22

The witness was named Janice Sheltenham. She wouldn't talk to me, but Dell had already deposed her. Between that and what the prosecution provided as part of discovery, I had a pretty good picture of the woman and what she claimed to have observed.

Sheltenham was a nurse, married, with two kids in college and one in high school. She worked nights at a local hospital because of the shift differential. Her husband, a machinist, worked nights at the Tesla plant in Fremont, also for the extra pay.

The couple coordinated their work schedules so they had the same nights off. The Friday Ruby Swanson lost her life was one of those nights. They also kept to the same routine each day so their bodies wouldn't go nuts; on their days off, they got up around 9 p.m. to start their day.

The night in question, Janice's morning, she said she was shopping at Dominici's. She was planning to prepare a special gourmet dinner for her dear husband, and preferred Dominici's meat, seafood, produce, and especially their bread. The store was several miles from her home, and there were any number of closer markets, but she said she made the drive when she was fixing something special. Dominici's *was* that kind of place.

Janice said she left the store as it was closing at 11 p.m. She was getting into her car, which happened to be parked on the other side of the wall, almost directly opposite Ruby's, when she saw and heard Ruby and Tim going at it.

According to Janice, she saw a woman hurrying towards a car, a man hot on her heels. He was yelling something about her leading him on, and she definitely heard "cockteaser."

Not being a nosey person, and not wanting to get involved with a couple of drunks, she backed out and drove home. But she distinctly remembered the woman standing with her back to the driver's car door and the man looming over her and screaming obscenities. The man seemed to be holding something in his left hand, but she was not sure of that. That last was a nice detail. Our client was left-handed, and the ME said the fatal blow was most likely left-handed.

Janice had picked Ruby out of a photo array and Tim out of a lineup. She described Ruby's car, a brown Sonata, reasonably well, though she could not be sure of the color, just that it was dark.

Asked why it had taken her over a week to come for-

Final Part

ward, she said she assumed at the time it was just another booze-driven argument and had no idea it had escalated to violence. She and her husband did not get the newspaper, nor did they watch local newscasts. The next week, when she was again at Dominici's, she heard someone talking about the murder next door the previous Friday. After discussing it with her husband, Janice decided she should talk to the police.

Janice could not say for sure that she had seen the weapon. She left before any blows were struck. But, instead of being flaws, Dell said not being uncertain about these sorts of details, like the color of the car, strengthened her credibility. She had only witnessed them for maybe a minute. A good attorney could usually destroy a witness whose memory was too good to be true on cross examination.

There was one flaw in Janice Sheltenham's account. Though her husband confirmed it, she could not otherwise prove she was at Dominici's on that night, at that time. She did not recall talking to anyone there or remember who checked her out. She had no register receipt and claimed she and her husband did not like to use checks or credit cards and mostly paid cash. She later produced bank and credit card statements to confirm that, and her credit report showed she had revealed all their accounts, which were few. She also had taken a photo of a stack of the distinctive white Dominici bags she kept on a shelf in the garage; she used them, she said, to line her kitchen trash and recycling bins.

*   *   *

I had pretty much verified that the lights in Widow O'Toole's lot were all working that night. The widow was nervous about being sued and authorized the maintenance company she used to talk to me. They came by monthly to do an inspection of the whole place and make minor repairs. One of the checklist items was parking lot lighting. They had been inspected and were working just days before the incident, and there had been no subsequent lighting problem reported.

I canvassed Janice Sheltenham's neighborhood and mostly got doors slammed in my face. I ran into the usual neighborhood snoop and gossip, but her only complaint was that the family parked their vehicles on the street because their garage was full of crap and they kept a small boat on a trailer in their driveway.

I checked out Janice's husband and kids. No police records. The older two were doing okay in college. The girl in high school got decent grades and was considered to be a good kid.

I did learn that Mr. Sheltenham had gone through a long stretch of unemployment a while back. The big manufacturer he had worked for had been one of the

Final Part

last in Silicon Valley until they, too, moved their California plants to lower cost states and countries. Things had been tough until he finally landed the graveyard shift job at the auto plant in Fremont when they ramped up production a couple of years ago.

I was working my ass off, putting in a lot of hours, all billable, but getting nowhere fast.

Chapter 23

I read about Suzy Lou's death while munching my mid-morning donut, in the local section of the *San Jose Mercury News*. The article was headlined "Local Realtor Dies in Maui Accident." It said she was way over the legal limit for alcohol and had driven off a cliff on a pitch-dark, treacherous section of road while on vacation. She had been alone.

I called the Maui police department and left a message for the detective handling the case. She called me later in the day. As with the Mayfair case, it was being treated as an open-and-shut accident. I got the same message I had gotten from Santa Clara County Detective Nicki Nguyen: call back if and when you have some hard evidence.

The subtext of our conversation was that it was better for tourism for the police to use the accident as part of their ongoing campaign against drunk driving than to call it a possible murder. No doubt, murder was bad for the tourist business.

Without Suzy, there would be no sketch of Graham Westonovic. It was time to focus on finding Stephanie

Final Part

Westonovic. She had not called me, despite the alluring message I had left with her mother.

I reminded myself that the only reason I was interested in Stephanie Westonovic was that she might get me to her cousin, Graham. And my interest in Graham was because he was somehow connected to Billy Mayfair through his new car. I was quite a bit away from my real quarry, but those were the leads I had.

I found myself wishing I could just get a DeepDig report on Graham Westonovic. For that matter, I would have liked reports on the Mayfairs, parents and son. DeepDig was an online service that extracted data from all sorts of databases, including many that they hacked into. Then a DeepDig employee integrated that data into a well-organized report and wrote a summary. DeepDigs were only available to attorneys, licensed private investigators, and law enforcement organizations. And they were expensive. I asked; the insurance company would not authorize the cost.

* * *

I had lunch with Dell Chamberlin. It was his introduction to Greasy Jack's, and I could tell he liked the place. Dell was down-to-earth, definitely not your snooty, white-shoe lawyer type.

While we waited for our orders to be ready, I briefed Dell on my progress, or lack of it, on the Conrad case. I asked if I could get DeepDigs on some of the key players. Once again, I struck out.

"Not a chance, Joe. That's way out of our client's price range." Which meant my paltry fees were within his price range. *Ah well.*

Our gadgets lit up and buzzed, and we went to pick up our food. While we ate, I asked Dell if he knew about stepped-up basis. It had been lurking in the back of my mind and had just sort of floated to the surface.

"Sure, it's an important part of estate planning. The short, simple answer is, if you sell your home, unless you roll the proceeds into the purchase of another home, you have to pay tax on the difference between what you sold it for and what it cost, which is called the basis, less any mortgage balance. That amount is the capital gain.

"But if you die, or, in the case of a couple, if you're the last to die, your estate gets to use the current market value of the property as the new basis. That's called the stepped-up basis. If the estate sells right away, there's no tax to pay. So, if you have much capital gain, which most people do, especially in Silicon Valley, it can help your heirs if you hold onto your home until you die. Tens or hundreds of thousands of dollars in taxes can be avoided."

Dell said there were all sorts of complicating details, but that was basically it.

I appreciated that Dell had refrained from legalese

Final Part

and lawyerly pontification. I asked a few questions and felt that I understood stepped-up basis.

"Why do you ask?"

"I think it may have something to do with the Mayfair case I mentioned to you when we first met," I said.

"How so?"

I decided to keep it short and sweet. "I have reason to believe the Mayfairs were murdered. The only one who had a motive was their druggy son who inherited everything. This stepped-up basis thing may be a factor."

"Well, if you ever want to talk more about it, let me know."

* * *

Back at the office after lunch, I plunged into Westonovic research. As is often the case, there were false trails and dead-ends in this kind of detecting. It was matter of separating the relevant from the irrelevant. The trick, or skill, as I preferred to think of it, was in figuring out which was which.

The puzzle pieces finally started coming together in the afternoon. The Westonovics were part of a good-sized Croatian community in Indianapolis. Hilda, now a widow, had been married to Graham's father's brother. Her daughter Stephanie and Graham were born in the same year, grew up on the same block, went to the same schools. At Indiana State, she was in the nursing program, he studied theater arts. After graduation, Graham headed for Hollywood. Cousin Stephanie married Vern Cunningham and moved to Mountain View. If she was still there, we were practically neighbors.

I went downstairs and got a glazed donut. I wanted to search online for Stephanie Cunningham, but glazed donuts shed sugary snowflakes which mess up a mouse and keyboard, so I took a break.

I got to thinking about Suzy Lou. Besides the timing, something about Suzy's accident bothered me, but I could not form it into a conscious thought. It was just a feeling, as insubstantial as mist. I remembered that I had helped Boomer pry information out of Suzy by keeping her wine glass full at lunch that day. I could see her getting plastered on vacation, missing a turn, and driving off a cliff.

I found it hard to picture that pretty, effervescent woman dead. I thought about how it didn't matter how animated she was in life. Dead is dead.

I licked my fingers, wondering at how yummy donuts and gloomy thoughts had gotten tangled together, and went back to the computer.

It took less than ten minutes to locate Stephanie Cunningham. It appeared that she still lived in Mountain View and worked for the county as a public health nurse.

Final Part

It was time to pay Nurse Cunningham a visit.

Chapter 24

Stephanie was enjoying a glass of wine after work, sitting barefoot in a comfortable chair she had positioned where the sun came in through the deck sliders in her condo. When her glass was empty, she closed her eyes and, catlike, absorbed the rays and let her thoughts drift.

After she had eliminated the Bimbo and the Bastard, Stephanie had been surprised to discover she had no feelings about it. Other than the satisfaction of revenge, that is. She had expected some sort of negative emotions like guilt and remorse, but they just weren't there. Instead, she experienced a sort of clinical detachment.

It made her wonder if she might be a sociopath, a person devoid of normal human emotions who is indifferent towards, if not finds enjoyment in, the pain of others. But she was not a violent person, never had been. She had never taken pleasure in causing others grief. Intellectually, she knew what she had done was wrong, but it just did not bother her. It was like she felt about exceeding the speed limit: nothing.

Final Part

She considered herself an honest, law-abiding person. She had never committed a crime before. When she wronged others, she generally felt regret, sometimes guilt. But this thing with Vern seemed somehow different. Righteous was the word that came to mind.

When she got the idea about how to get rich from the new Medicare program for socially isolated seniors, it had surprised her that she could contemplate killing an elderly person or couple to get their wealth. *No,* she thought, *not get. Steal. Call it what it is.* Bad? Yes. Wrong. Yes. But not bad or wrong enough not to do it. It would set her up for the life she felt she deserved, the life she would have had if the Bastard had not been such a bastard.

She got the idea after a training session for the Medicare senior support program. The instructor mentioned, almost as an aside, that one of the problems confronting many seniors in Silicon Valley was that they had most of their wealth tied up in their home equity. This was because of the crazy price increases that had driven the average home price to over a million dollars. That was average, which meant many homes were now worth a lot more. Many elderly people, often of modest means, had bought many years ago and had hundreds of thousands, if not millions of dollars in home equity.

What got Stephanie's attention was the brief discussion of the conflict this could cause between elderly parents and their children. The old folks wanted to sell and use the proceeds to support themselves in their twilight years. That meant paying substantial capital gains taxes on the profit, but that was the cost of cashing in. However, if they did not sell, when they died their heirs would not have to pay any capital gains because of something in the tax code called stepped-up basis.

The bottom line was that the heirs wanted mom and dad to hold onto the property to avoid the tax man. Hundreds of thousands of dollars, perhaps millions, of inheritance could be at stake.

Greedy buggers, she had thought at the time. But that brief discussion planted the seed of an idea. As it grew and flowered, she began looking for the right situation.

And find the right situation she did. The Mayfairs were one of several of her assigned cases she had investigated before the first home visit. She was looking for a person or couple who were isolated, wealthy, and, most important, had a single heir she could manipulate, to whose greed she could appeal.

The pitch would be simple. The old folks want to cash in, spend all their money before they die, leave the heir whatever paltry sum remained. But if they died now, the heir would get a windfall, and she, Stephanie, could make all that happen.

The Mayfairs had fit the profile. It seemed likely that

Final Part

they had a ton of cash tied up in their home, and their only heir was their errant, estranged son, who lived three thousand miles away.

But how would she communicate with him and convince him to join the conspiracy that included murdering his parents? That was always the weak part of her scheme, one she had postponed dealing with in detail. When she discovered that Billy Mayfair was a lowlife ex-con who had heartlessly swindled his parents several times and was in a drug diversion program, she saw the way.

Stephanie had done a lot of research on the Mayfairs before meeting with them. Then she began their sessions, during which she verified her assumptions. The more she learned about their situation, the more certain she was that this was the opportunity she had been looking for, one too good to let pass. She had already primed Graham; she put the plan into motion.

As kids, she and her cousin had been inseparable. She had sensed that he was gay early on, but it was not a subject to broach in their conservative family. While she dated men and then got engaged to Vern in college, Graham kept his love life under wraps.

Stephanie had not been surprised when Graham split right after graduation. It was bad enough that he wanted to be an actor, but he was off to that den of iniquity, Hollywood. By that time, his sexuality, the sin that was at the root of familial dismay, was an open family secret; everyone knew but no one spoke of it.

Graham's acting career took off when he landed a major supporting part in a new soap opera. He looked great and was adept at taking direction and getting into character, but he was missing a crucial skill: he could not memorize his lines and became tongue-tied reading them off a prompter.

Thus, his character was written out of the show halfway through the first season. Word got around, and soon the only parts he could get were those without dialog. He would even struggle to handle one-liners.

Years passed. Graham scraped by. He was offered modelling opportunities, took some, but his heart wasn't in it. He was an actor. When he realized he was going nowhere, he turned to private acting.

It was a perfect fit. Graham was given a character to play. After that, it was all improv. He excelled at staying in character and playing the part.

Graham gave up his apartment and bought a used RV that became his home. He could live cheaply, near his private engagements, which soon were coming in from all over the West Coast.

The sound of her doorbell chiming interrupted Stephanie's reverie.

Chapter 25

It was after 5:30 when I drove down Campbell Avenue, made a left onto Winchester Boulevard, and got onto 85 just across from Netflix headquarters, heading north to Mountain View. It was rush hour, and the freeway traffic going in the other direction was bumper to bumper. But I had clear sailing.

Twenty minutes later, I parked on the street in a tract of well-maintained, attached condos in a middle-income Mountain View neighborhood. I located the Cunningham residence, went up two steps to a small porch, and pressed the doorbell.

I had not called ahead. It's easier for people to dodge you over the phone than in person or just hang up. If they agree to meet, the call gives them time to prepare their story, or even decide to be out or just not answer the door when you show up. Assuming Stephanie's mother gave her my message and she had chosen to ignore it, I decided the personal approach was in order, and took the chance that I'd catch someone home at 6 p.m.

A barefoot, drowsy-looking woman opened the door

a few inches.

"Can I help you?"

"I hope so. I'm looking for Stephanie Cunningham. My name's Joe Brink."

I held out my card. She opened the door a bit wider, took the card, read it, looked puzzled.

"A private investigator?"

"Yes, ma'am. Are you Stephanie Cunningham?"

She nodded.

"Was your maiden name Westonovic?"

She nodded again, probably reflexively.

"I wonder if I might have a moment of your time."

She blinked a few times. "What's this about?"

"May I come in, please? It'll only take a few minutes."

"You can tell me what this is about or leave. Your choice." The sleepiness was gone.

"I'm trying to locate your cousin Graham. I was told you might know how I could get in touch with him."

By this time, the door was open. She stood in the doorway, firmly blocking entrance. Voice firm, she said, "Last chance, Mr. Brink. What about?"

Ignoring the testiness, I smiled my most accommodating smile, as if her request were entirely reasonable. "Graham's name came up in connection with a case I'm working on. I need to ask him a few questions about a friend of his. I'm afraid I'm not at liberty to go into the details."

Final Part

That "I'm not at liberty" line usually works wonders. I'm not sure why. Maybe because it sounds official. Stephanie, however, was unimpressed.

"Well, that's too bad."

I sensed she was about to close the door. I had one more ploy, but before I could try it, she asked, "Do you know a Cole Spenser?"

Keep her talking. "Yes, I do. He's also working on the case."

She nodded, as if my answer had confirmed something. "Look, Mr. Brink, let me save us both some time. I don't know how to reach Graham, haven't heard from him in months. He's like a gypsy, moves around a lot, and we really don't keep in touch. I'm afraid I can't help you."

I used my last ploy. "Well, thanks for your time. I was hoping not to need to go to the police about this, but I guess I have no choice."

"I guess you don't," she said, and closed the door. As if to punctuate our conversation, I heard the dead bolt click into place.

* * *

The alias I used, Cole Spenser, was a tribute to the fictional PIs who were my role models, Robert Crais's Elvis Cole and the late Robert B. Parker's Spenser. I had tried two tactics they both often used, charm and intimidation. Stephanie Westonovic Cunningham had been impervious to those tactics. As I drove away, I wondered what my heroes would do next.

Probably nothing, I decided. Elvis and Spenser both liked to poke the nest and then wait and see what the hornets would do. I had poked Stephanie and my hunch was that either she or Graham would call soon.

Only later did I realize I had made two mistakes. First, I should have investigated Stephanie a bit more before approaching her. I would probably not have discovered the connection to the Mayfair's, but I would have easily found out about the murders of her ex-husband and his pregnant fiancée, and that would have been a red flag, warning me to proceed cautiously.

My second miscalculation was that calling me was not the only possible response Stephanie or Graham might make. Angry hornets were unpredictable.

* * *

The memorial for Suzy Lou was filled with energetic 30-somethings who I took to be her friends. They were telling Suzy stories and the too-hearty laughter that accompanies remembering the dead filled the room.

Off to the side sat an older Chinese-looking couple who were obviously Suzy's parents. They appeared to still be in shock at the senseless loss of their daughter. They were guarded by a phalanx of somber looking

Final Part

mourners. These were surely their immediate family and closest friends. This group spoke only in hushed voices.

I wasn't sure why I had stopped in, but it seemed important. I left without speaking to anyone.

Chapter 26

Shit! Shit, shit, shit, shit, shit.

Stephanie leaned with her back against her closed front door. Her stomach cramped, and she wanted to scream out loud. Instead, she did so silently.

Her skin felt clammy. Her thoughts began racing, along with her heart and breathing. She knew the symptoms of a panic attack, knew she had to calm down so she could think rationally. She had helped patients do so; helping herself was far more difficult.

She focused on slowing her breathing. Deep, even breaths. Think about nothing but that. Slowly, she gained control. Her heart began to slow. The lightheadedness receded.

After what seemed like an hour but was just a couple of minutes, Stephanie felt able to move. She went into the bathroom, opened the medicine cabinet, and swallowed a couple of Valiums. Then she went into her bedroom and laid down on her back on the made bed.

Drowsiness soon won out over anxiety, and she drifted off.

Final Part

* * *

In the morning, Stephanie called in sick. She made herself a comforting breakfast of pancakes and sausages, the latter dug from the bottom of the freezer. After she ate and cleared the table, she got a pad and pen and sat down with a second cup of coffee to get her thoughts in order.

They were so close, she thought. In just a matter of days, they would close on the real estate sale, the online investment firm would release the Mayfair accounts, and a day later, all the money would be sitting in the accounts she had set up for herself and Graham.

She would hand in her resignation, apologize for not giving notice because of a family emergency, and head for Provence, where she would purchase an old farmhouse, maybe take in stray dogs and cats, an eccentric American woman gossiped about by the French villagers.

After her condo sold, she would add another million dollars to her nest egg. She had at least gotten that out of the divorce settlement.

Graham planned to return to L.A. and open an acting school. He was, after all, a good actor. He just had a mental block when it came to memorizing or reading scripted lines.

After returning from Maui, Stephanie had thought she might have overreacted about the photo of Suzy

Lou with Graham's new car. Now she thought otherwise. Graham's wiseass carelessness coupled with Joe Brink and Cole Spenser sniffing around were sure signs that things could unravel.

Except for the car blunder, Graham had been doing a fantastic job. He had, as planned, gone completely off the grid. No credit card use, no checks, no way to track him. He drove to New York, where he found and cased Billy Mayfair. As soon as Billy got out of rehab, he kidnapped him. He got a few bits of critical information along with his phone and driver's license from him, killed him and disposed of the body.

Then it was time for his Academy Award performance. Graham Westonovic played the part of Billy Mayfair. Dressed like him. Groomed, or, more like failed to groom himself, like him. Spoke a streetwise patois. Went to Queens where he could get lost among the anonymous millions, rented a hovel, got the sort of job Billy could do, and waited.

When the cop called to inform him of his parents' deaths, lowlife Billy Mayfair pulled himself together, cleaned up his act and came home to do his duty.

On the top of the page, she wrote: **Keep close tabs on G**. Under that, she added: **Find out what Spenser and Brink want**.

She knew this could no longer be dealt with by acting autonomously and communicating with text messages. They had to work the endgame together. They had to

Final Part

trade the risk of meeting for the greater risk of things falling apart.

She added one last item to her list: **Meet with G**.

Chapter 27

Until Janice Sheltenham came forward, the cops were all over Ruby Swanson's ex. And for good reason. He was prime suspect material, except for one small detail. He had an excellent alibi.

I got great background on Kevin Hill from the sitter who Ruby had been rushing home to relieve. Briana Brisco had been Janice's best friend since they were cheerleaders in high school. We had a long lunch at a nice seafood place just a block from my office. I even ordered a bottle of white wine. Tim Conrad was footing the bill.

Kevin Hill and Ruby Swanson had gone to high school together. Kevin, an average student, was a popular star athlete and class president. Ruby was perpetually on the honor roll and head cheerleader. They were prom king and queen. The perfect couple.

Kevin's problem was that high school would turn out to be the high point of his life. It was all downhill after graduation, and the slope was steep.

Ruby's problem was that, pregnant, she married Kevin just a few weeks after graduation, then had two

Final Part

kids in rapid succession.

Kevin had not been college material academically, and his athletic prowess brought no offers of a college scholarship. He proceeded to fail as a car salesman, insurance salesman, aluminum siding salesman, and was soon struggling to find a trade that would take advantage of the only skill he seemed to possess, one that no longer impressed his wife: he was good with his hands. Kevin finally caught on as an apprentice for an HVAC outfit. It was a job he managed to hold, and he became proficient. After two years, he became a journeyman. It would be his last promotion.

What with the kids and a flakey husband, by the time Ruby was able to look around and take stock of her life, five years had passed. She decided things had to change. She was fed up with pinching pennies, their shithole apartment, the thrift shop clothes she and the kids wore, and their dangerous neighborhood and underachieving schools. Truth be told, she was also fed up with Kevin, but was unwilling to admit that to herself quite yet. That would come later.

Ruby got a job as a marketing assistant at a tech startup. She was hired because she was literate, knew her way around a computer, coaxed a great reference from one of her high school teachers, and worked cheap. She loved the adult company. She loved the air of excitement. And the steady paycheck was not bad, either.

Ruby still managed to take care of the kids, do the housework, and get home in time to prepare Kevin's dinner. The latter chore was eased by his usual late arrival. He played ball in the evening twice a week, basketball in the winter, softball in the summer. On other nights, he had the habit of stopping off at his favorite dive bar after work to unwind.

On the weekends, while Ruby caught up on housework and took the kids to the park, Kevin watched sports on TV, drank beer, and laughed along with the parade of mindlessly chattering ex-jocks on the sports channels.

Meanwhile, Ruby's role grew as the startup grew. By the time they went public, she was director of marketing, no longer working for peanuts. As part of the IPO process, they brought in an industry veteran as Senior VP of marketing and sales to bolster their executive creds. Right after the IPO, he named Ruby as his VP of marketing. Her compensation had more than tripled since she started working.

One day, as she was paying the bills—her job, Kevin was no good with numbers, money, or record-keeping—Ruby had an epiphany. Kevin, whose income Ruby's dwarfed, cost more than he made. Put another way, she calculated that if she shed him, she and the kids would come out ahead financially. She spent a few days with the idea and realized she would experience no other loss. She doubted the kids would, either, but

Final Part

if they did, she was certain they would soon get over it.

Applying her business skills, Ruby made a project plan. Then she executed it. She hired a good lawyer and was single in a matter of months. Kevin insisted he didn't need a lawyer, so he got screwed. Ruby got full custody and control over visitation. She asked for no child support. Kevin was too proud to ask for alimony. He got his old truck and personal items. She got her new Toyota and everything else.

Ruby went back to her maiden name. Lacking a down payment, she negotiated a rent-to-own deal on a nice condo in a good neighborhood and moved across town.

Kevin was a charming, friendly man. Indifferent and inattentive to his family, not terribly bright, but a nice, easygoing guy. Except when he got drunk. This had rarely happened when they were married, but that changed after the divorce. He had not bothered to read any of the divorce paperwork. The man who had never had time to spend with his children was shocked when he realized that Ruby was in complete control of visitation. He was outraged when she refused to let him come by for sex. These affronts to his manhood became festering wounds. He drank more and more.

And when he drank, Kevin became angry and belligerent. He began showing up uninvited at Ruby's new home, sometimes in the evening, sometimes on the weekend. Banging on the door, screaming, demanding to be let in.

Neighbors who objected to the disturbance in their tranquil neighborhood were threatened with extreme bodily harm. Police were called. Several times, Kevin cooled his heels in the backseat of a police car until he calmed down, then was sent home in a taxi. The incidents escalated in frequency and severity. Restraining orders were secured.

As soon as he sobered up, he would become mild mannered Kevin. He could not remember, did not believe, accounts of drunken Kevin's behavior, even when shown video of an episode. Threatened by a judge with imprisonment, he vowed to get a grip. He enlisted a couple of drinking buddies to take away his keys when he started raging. Things settled down. By the time Ruby Swanson died, it had been nearly a year without a major Kevin episode.

Briana's parting words were, "When the cops came by and told me Ruby had been killed, my first thought was Kevin. I know he has an alibi, but I still think he did it. I hope you nail the fucker."

Chapter 28

Kevin Hill's favorite haunt was a bar in what the chamber of commerce would laughingly call a transitional neighborhood, meaning it was on a block with a mixture of decrepit industrial buildings and houses that longed for a wrecking ball.

The one-story, flat-roofed building was painted a faded black, windows included. It was surrounded by an unmarked, put-'em-where-you-can, gravel parking area. It was nearly anonymous, save for the small red neon sign over the door that proclaimed "Baldy's." It may as well have read, "Dive Bar-Swill on Tap."

The floorplan and general layout at Baldy's were similar to that of Widow O'Toole's. It was, I thought, a standard bar template. But that was where the similarities between the two drinking establishments ended.

Baldy's was lit mainly by lights over the two pool tables in the back and the glare of the jukebox. The bar was lined with unmovable stools—lest they became weapons in fights—topped with cracked black leatherette. Well-scratched black wooden booths lined the opposite wall. The worn floor was, yes, black, and sticky.

The place smelled of stale beer, cigarettes and marijuana.

I arrived late in the afternoon, before the after-work crowd started filtering in. There were a couple of gray-haired geezers sitting next to each other at the bar, beers in front of them. One booth was occupied by four younger men enjoying a pitcher of beer and a sharing a pizza. A woman on the juke box lamented about the cowboy who broke her heart.

I took a seat at the bar, leaving a few stools between myself and the old men. The bartender, a short, wiry guy with a shiny bald head, broke away from his conversation with the geezers. *Hello, Baldy.*

"What'll you have?"

"What kind of beer do you have?"

"Bud on tap."

"That's it?"

"That's it."

"I'll have a Bud."

I detected that this was not Widow O'Toole's, with its vast array of craft beers and ales.

Kevin Hill's alibi was that he had been banging Cora Corcoran in the back of her van in the parking lot at the time his ex-wife was killed. Cora served tables at Baldy's from 5 p.m. until closing. She supported Kevin's story. Several patrons saw them leave and return together. Baldy told the cops Nora routinely took her break from 10:30 to 11:00 but he had asked her to

Final Part

skip it that night because the other server had called in sick and the place was packed. But she insisted on taking the break at the appointed time, telling him to have the other bartender serve for a while, and Baldy was pissed off at her.

The time mattered. Ruby had been killed between 11:00 and 11:15 p.m., when the 9-1-1 call was logged. There was no way Kevin could have gotten across town to Widow O'Toole's and killed Ruby if he had been with Cora until 11:00.

I nursed my beer. At the dot of five o'clock, Cora and the second bartender arrived, and the place began to fill up. It was a working-class crowd, mostly men. Kevin, easily recognizable from the photo Dell had given me, came in with three big guys and they commandeered a booth. They were all wearing light blue shirts with Valley HVAC embroidered over the front pocket.

The pool tables were soon all in use, and raucous laughter competed with the country music blaring from the jukebox. Smoking was done openly. There were even plastic ash trays. Baldy's was apparently stuck in the last century, before California had banned smoking in bars.

Cora was what my mother would have called a full-figured girl. She looked to be in her 40s, had big bleached-blonde hair, wore a tight T-shirt and jeans, and was chummy with her customers.

I ate a slice of yucky, soggy pizza, then started on a second beer. I struck up a conversation with a guy who took the stool on my left. He was at least 70, with a full head of nearly white hair in a buzzcut and wore an army jacket that looked decades old. When he took his order, Baldy called him Sarge.

"Army, huh?" I said, looking straight ahead.

"Long time ago."

"Nam?"

"Nam."

And so it went. He said his name was Stan Zampisi. We chatted, random miscellaneous guy talk, slow and easy. After a while, I steered the conversation to the waitress.

"You mean, 'Cora, let's explore 'er.'" She was not really a hooker, Sarge said, but word was that a $100 tip could induce Cora to use her break for a romantic interlude. "Not that I know first-hand, know what I mean?"

After a couple of hours, I used the disgusting john, put my twenty on the edge of the pool table, took my turn against the prevailing winner, was a good loser. Waiting for 10:30.

As though responding to an internal alarm, Cora walked down the back hallway at exactly 10:30. I headed in the direction of the john and followed her out back. She was sitting in her van with the window open, eating a sub sandwich.

Final Part

I made a U-turn, strolled back inside, through the bar, out the front door, and headed for my Prius. I had gotten what I'd come for, but my night was not quite over.

* * *

I had parked on the street, concerned that I would get blocked in as the unlined parking lot filled. I walked across the lot. I never made it to my car.

I heard footsteps behind me and turned as two guys came up to me. They were Kevin Hill's bar buddies, Big and Bigger. Big, who was the smallest and still had me by at least four inches and 50 pounds, said, "You been asking about Cora?"

I turned to run and crashed into the third brute, Biggest, who had come up behind me from between the haphazardly parked cars and trucks. I heard Big growl, "Stay away." Then they beat the crap out of me.

* * *

I came to in the back of an ambulance. I was on my back, strapped into a gurney. An EMT was leaning over me. "Don't try to get up," she said. "You've taken quite a beating, but you're in good hands now." Fade to black.

Next thing I knew, I was in a hospital bed in a

brightly lit room. "He's coming around," a male voice said.

My vision began clearing. A pretty woman with an Indian lilt in her voice came into focus. "Mr. Brink, can you hear me?"

"Yes," I croaked. My throat felt like sandpaper.

"You've taken quite a beating."

I was pretty sure I had heard that same phrase what seemed like just a moment ago.

"You have cuts, an impressive selection of hematomas, cracked ribs and a broken arm. Also a concussion. But we've put you back together and you're going to be fine. You have some excellent pain medication."

"Thank you. Water?"

"Right away. I'll let your visitors know they can come in."

The male nurse cranked me up to a sitting position and let me sip water through a straw. My head hurt, but I wasn't dizzy, more like fuzzy, probably from the drugs they had administered.

Anna and Sally were soon at my bedside. Anna took my hand and looked like she was going to cry. Sally looked pissed. "We gotta talk," Sally said.

My fictional heroes Spenser and Elvis Cole are hard-boiled detectives. They're tough, good with their fists and, when needed, guns. I, however, was decidedly soft-boiled. I had met Sally after getting beaten up more than once at my former employer, Kowalski-Wu

Final Part

investigations. Sally taught self-defense and took me on as a project.

As for weapons, I was afraid of guns. But not just when others pointed them at me; I was certain that, were I to have one, I'd be the one who it would end up shooting.

Sally taught self-defense, what she called the escape and survive method, mainly to women who might need to protect themselves from men. Now she was on my case.

"You didn't escape, and you barely survived. As soon as you're well enough, I'm putting you in my advanced class."

"I didn't know you had an advanced class."

"I do now."

* * *

The next morning, a young cop came by to take my statement. I told him I'd stopped in at Baldy's, had a couple of beers, played some pool and left. Blaming the concussion, I said I had no memory of the fight. Not true, but I could always claim to have recovered it later if needed.

"Who'd you piss off while you were there?"

"No one. I didn't know anyone there, either."

"You go to Baldy's often?"

"First time."

"You might want to find a better place to drink."
"Good advice."

He put his notebook away, then I had a thought. "Who made the 9-1-1 call?"

He flipped open the notebook. "Guy's name is Stan Zampisi. Found you on the ground when he went out to his car."

I was pretty sure that I had heard something like that before in this case, too. Parking lots could be dangerous places.

* * *

Boomer came by around lunch time with a Greasy Jack's bag containing a cheeseburger, fries and a milkshake. Now I would recover my strength.

He also had Sarge, a.k.a. Stan Zampisi, with him. Even from my hospital bed, I had been detecting. I'd used my phone to look up Sarge's address and phone number, then asked Boomer to try to find him. I knew he was retired and guessed he'd be home in the morning. I was right.

"Thanks for rescuing me," I said.

"Wish I'd been able to move faster," Sarge said. "I thought Baldy was kind of listening in on us. Soon as you left, he went over to Hill's table, and his asshole buddies went right out after you. I knew they were up to no good, but these old legs only go so fast. By the

Final Part

time I got there, you were out cold and they were gone."

I thought that had probably been a good thing for Sarge. I don't think he'd have stopped the big guys and would likely have been hurt trying.

Chapter 29

I had a cast on my left arm and a strict concussion regimen to follow, but I was back on the job.

While I was in the hospital, DeepDig had gone out of business. More accurately, they had been put out of business. Two things doomed the service. First, a judge had thrown a murder case out of court because the cops had used a DeepDig report to help direct their investigation. The judge ruled that using a report that stated upfront that some of its contents may have been illegally obtained violated the defendant's constitutional rights.

The second and perhaps more damning blow came when it was revealed that DeepDig was using report requests to blackmail well-off subjects. They would contact the person and, for a hefty sum, allow them to edit the report before it was delivered to the customer who had ordered the report.

Authorities from several countries were after the people who ran DeepDig, and the Indian government had shut them down.

Final Part

* * *

Four days had passed and not a peep from Stephanie or Graham. I was feeling snubbed. More importantly, I was stuck on the case. Every path I'd taken had turned into a dead-end, and Indira Kapoor was pressing me for progress, if not results.

I was sitting at my desk just after nine o'clock, taking a break from the Conrad case and contemplating my next move on the Mayfair case, when my office door opened, and a thin black man walked in. He wore a blue sport coat over an open-collared blue dress shirt and gray slacks. As he took in my spartan office, his face said that what he saw did not please him.

"Can I help you?"

"Are you Joe Brink?"

"I am."

"I'm Detective Taylor with the San Jose Police. I'd like to ask you a few questions."

I noticed Taylor had what appeared to be a permanent squint. It gave his face a skeptical quality. I motioned for him to sit down. He closed the door and eyed my guest chairs distastefully. I don't know why. They're in good condition and clean.

As he sat down, I said, "Can I see your creds?" I liked calling his ID creds. Joe Brink, gritty PI. They said his name was LeBarton Taylor. He looked to be in his late 50s or early 60s and reminded me of the character Ice-

T plays on *Law and Order: SVU*, only less weather-beaten.

"How can I help you, detective?"

"Do you know a Stephanie Cunningham?"

"Her name came up in one of my cases. I spoke to her once."

"Spoke to how?"

"I stood on her front porch a few days ago. She stood in the doorway. We spoke briefly. She did not invite me inside."

His eyes went from the bandage on my head to the cast on my arm. "She do that to you?"

"I had an altercation in the parking lot of a bar a couple of days ago. Unrelated."

His skeptical eye twitched. "What did you speak about?"

"Care to tell me why you're asking?"

"That isn't how this works," Taylor said. "I ask; you answer."

I remembered a Spenser technique. I smiled my friendliest smile and said nothing. Detective Taylor did not smile back. His squint became more pronounced. I stood and headed for my little fridge.

"Care for a Coke? I have diet or high-test. Or maybe water or coffee?"

Taylor expelled an "it's gonna be one of those days" sigh. "I checked you out, Brink. You're still wet behind the ears, but Curt Kowalski says you're okay, so I'm

Final Part

gonna cut you some slack. I'll take a Diet Coke."

We popped our soda cans, sipped, dialed down the testosterone and reset the conversation.

"The body of Stephanie Cunningham was found last night in the trunk of a car in the long-term parking lot at San Jose Airport. She had been shot once in the back of the head."

I felt my cool demeanor slipping. "How did you get to me?"

"We found your card on her kitchen counter."

At least she hadn't thrown it away. I wanted to know more, but knew it was time for me to give Taylor something in exchange.

"I spoke to her Thursday at about six o'clock. Like I said, I didn't get past the front door. I was looking for her cousin and asked if she knew how I could get in touch with him. She said she didn't and shut the door in my face."

A notebook and pen appeared. Taylor jotted something. "What was this cousin's name?"

"Graham Westonovic. Also goes by Graham West. Stephanie Cunningham's maiden name was Westonovic. They grew up together."

Taylor's right eye twitched. "What's your interest in this guy?"

"Can you tell me more about the circumstances of her death?"

Taylor looked away, did some calculating, came to a

decision. "The car was a new BMW convertible..."

I interrupted. "Red, registered to Graham Westonovic."

It appeared to take considerable effort, but the corners of Taylor's lips rose imperceptibly to form a thin, tight smile. "How do you know that?"

"I'll tell you in a minute. How was she found?"

"Some kids tried to steal the car. What they do is drive into the lot, drive around looking for something worth stealing. When they find a likely target, one of them gets out to check it out. The plan is to hotwire the car and pay the parking fee on the way out. People tend to leave the ticket in the car. Anyway, before he does anything, the kid pops the trunk. Said he didn't want to get caught with drugs or something. Saw the body, called 9-1-1. Then took off with his buddies. Thing is, we got them on a security camera tear-assing out of the lot and picked them up during the night. We'll cut them some slack because of the 9-1-1 call."

"I don't suppose the killer left the gun."

"You don't suppose correctly."

"Killed elsewhere, then put in the trunk?"

"Looks like it."

It was my turn. "I'm working on an insurance case." I explained that the insurance company wanted me to investigate the Mayfairs' deaths before paying on the life and ADD policies. I also mentioned Boomer's suspicions, and that it was me who had solicited the case

Final Part

from the insurance company. I could think of no reason to withhold any of that.

"I was trying to find the son, Billy Mayfair. The realtor who sold the house told us that he was driving this new, red, BMW convertible. I found out that the only such car that was sold recently was bought by Graham Westonovic. I wanted to find him to find Billy Mayfair. That led me to Stephanie Cunningham." I also told him about the Fremont postal box Graham had used as an address.

Taylor nodded. He understood about following breadcrumbs. He probably already knew the address was a dead-end.

"Who is this realtor?"

"Her name was Suzy Lou."

"Was?"

"She died in Maui last week. They said it was an accident."

I got the squint again. "You are a fount of useful information."

Fount? I went for gritty, he's going for literate? "I just keep investigating; things turn up."

"I know how that is," Taylor said. "What will you do now?"

"I don't know," I said, "but I'm even more interested in locating Graham Westonovic and Billy Mayfair."

"As am I. Are you willing to share?"

"As long as it really goes both ways," I said.

Another strained smile. "I'll do what I can."

In our new spirit of cooperation, he reached inside his jacket and took a folded sheet of paper out of his pocket. It looked like a photocopy of a sheet of lined paper.

Keep close tabs on G
Find out what Spenser and Brink want
Meet with G

"This is a copy of a note we found next to your business card," Taylor said, "Who's Spenser?"

* * *

After Detective Taylor left, I called Santa Clara County Detective Nicki Nguyen. Surprisingly, I reached her directly. "I have something more substantial."

"I bet you say that to all the girls."

"Only when it's true," I said.

"And what might this be about?"

"Remember the Mayfairs?"

"Drowned in a car accident in Lexington Reservoir? You think it was murder?"

"That's them."

I swear I could hear her eyes roll. Or maybe it was just a sigh. "What do you have?"

"I suggest you call Detective Taylor at SJPD and ask

Final Part

him."

"Bart Taylor? How's he involved?"

"Just call him." I was being a fount.

Chapter 30

I had told Detective Taylor about my difficulty finding a photo of Billy Mayfair. The next day, he emailed me a copy of Billy's mug shot that he had received from New York.

That was a good sign. My experience with police sharing information had not been good. They seemed to think it was a one-way street. You gave, they took. When they did cough something up, it was not to be completely trusted; they had at times shaped what they revealed to me to manipulate me for some agenda they had.

I had no illusions that Taylor would let me inside his case. It was a cop's nature to be distrustful of others and keep an investigation under wraps. Still, I hoped to get a few useful scraps. Like the photo.

Taylor had asked me to keep what I suspected about the connections among the Mayfair, Westonovic and Lou deaths to myself for now. He and Detective Nguyen thought it would be better at this stage of their investigation to keep the bad guys, and thus the news media, in the dark about what they knew. Thus, the article in

Final Part

the morning paper only stated that Stephanie Cunningham had been found dead from a bullet wound in the trunk of her cousin's car, and that Graham Westonovic was wanted for questioning.

It was tit-for-tat. I got the photo, I kept what I knew from the press. I agreed.

* * *

"As you predicted, I just had a nice chat with your friend Detective Taylor," Boomer said as he walked into my office. "Thanks for the heads-up."

Boomer held a small white bag. He put it on my desk and carefully opened it. Two apple-crumb donuts. The smell was delicious. "These just came out of the oven downstairs."

We both popped sodas from my fridge and enjoyed our snacks while they were still warm.

"I'm going over to the Sheriff's Department later to talk to Detective Nguyen," Boomer said. "Seems she and Taylor had a little chat. They're taking another look at the so-called accident."

"So now we have two police departments looking into it. That's progress."

"I guess. But we also have a couple more dead bodies. What the hell do you think is going on?"

I was chewing my last mouthful of apple-crumb. I slid the note Taylor had given me across the desk.

**Keep close tabs on G
Find out what Spenser and Brink want
Meet with G**

"They found this in Stephanie Cunningham's condo," I said, sweeping the crumbs off my desk and into my hand. "She must have written it after I saw her. Anyway, I took my morning run today with my neighbors, Jonathan and Charles. Which got me wondering, what if Billy and Graham are a couple?"

Boomer nodded. "Lots of actors are gay."

"It could also account for Billy not fitting in at school or at home. Maybe his parents didn't even know, or maybe that was what first alienated them."

"Could be. The bigger the city, the bigger the gay scene. Nothing bigger than New York."

"It fits what we know and would explain some things. But we have no direct evidence of a relationship," I said. "Or how cousin Stephanie fits in. We detectives have to be careful about talking ourselves into a narrative."

"We?"

"That's the editorial we. As in me."

"Dang, and here I thought I'd been deputized or something." Boomer glanced at the newspaper on my desk, did a double-take and pointed to the headline. "Jesus! 'Mob-Style Hit at Airport!' And they don't even

Final Part

know about the Mayfair connection."

"If they get wind of Billy Mayfair's criminal record, they'll go apeshit," I said. "It's the never-ending quest for readership. But the mob thing is possible."

"Along with the gay-couple angle?"

"At this point, I have no idea. One thing for sure, Graham would not have left Stephanie's body in his own car like that. It's like putting up a billboard asking the cops to come after him. Plus, it was an expensive, brand new car."

"If it was a mob hit, maybe they're sending him a message."

I wondered if Boomer had watched too many TV cop shows. On the other hand, he might be right. This case just kept getting weirder.

Chapter 31

I had been cooling my heels for ten minutes in a SJPD interview room. Detective Taylor had called and asked me to come in. More like summoned than asked.

Taylor and Sheriff's Detective Nicki Nguyen walked in and sat across from me. That was unusual, working across jurisdictions that way, but they looked comfortable with each other. I assumed the two had worked together before and developed trust.

I decided to take the initiative. "Are we still sharing, or am I a suspect?"

"I'm investigating the airport murder," Taylor said. "Detective Nguyen is investigating the deaths of Sharon and Thomas Mayfair. You seem to link these crimes together. We want to know everything you know."

Everyone knows you shouldn't talk to the cops without your lawyer present. In my business, that doesn't work. I deal with cops too much; I'd spend all my income on legal fees. I already had a good track record with Detective Nguyen and it would be good to develop a positive relationship with Detective Taylor. I decided

Final Part

not to lawyer up.

"I think you already know what I know. But go ahead and ask your questions."

They did. Methodically, for almost an hour. I gave them everything they asked, because I could not think of a good reason not to. At that point, all our interests were aligned.

"Okay," Taylor said. "I think that does it."

"Not so fast," I said.

"You got something else?"

"How about we take a bathroom break and maybe you can get me a Coke? Then we'll see?"

Ten minutes later, I had my can of Coke and we were back together.

"What you got?" Taylor said.

"Just a couple of questions. Remember, we're sharing?"

They exchanged glances, then nods. "Go ahead, Joe," Nguyen said. "Ask,"

"What about the Suzy Lou murder? Any progress in Maui?"

"They're still calling it an accident," she said.

"Okay, one more thing. Like you said, I gave you the link between these cases." I looked at Nguyen. "I like to think I got you to reopen the Mayfair case." I shifted my gaze to Taylor. "But I know what I gave you was weak and you wouldn't just take it at face value. The thing is, from the questions you've asked, it sounds like you're sure about the connection."

I let that hang there. I had not asked a question, but I had opened the cooperation door. More glances and nods. Then Taylor dropped the first bomb. "Stephanie Cunningham was a public health nurse working for a program serving seniors. Sharon and Thomas Mayfair were one of her open cases."

Well!

"There's more," Nguyen said. "She may have been the last person to see the Mayfairs alive. She has an appointment with them late that afternoon. We had found it on their calendar and spoken to her, but she said it had been a routine appointment and they were fine when she left. The interview with her was filed away. Remember, we thought it was an accident. That interview was just a formality."

* * *

As I drove to the BMW dealership, I wondered if I was killing people, albeit indirectly. I met with Suzy Lou; she was dead. I met with Stephanie Cunningham; she was dead. I knew in my business it was easy to make that leap when instead of being a player you were just sticking your nose into things that were moving along without your help, more like watching the play instead of acting in it. Still, I wondered if I should warn Hector Lopez.

Final Part

Nah. If I started thinking like that, I couldn't do my job.

I had called and told the car salesman I was a detective but left out the "private" part. I offered to buy Hector lunch, but he declined, saying he couldn't afford to be away that long and miss a sales opportunity. He agreed to give me five minutes and meet outside on the lot.

If Billy Mayfair and Graham Westonovic were a couple, maybe they had shopped for the car together, like Anna and I shopped for furniture. A long shot, but it seemed worth taking a half hour to check it out.

Hector Lopez was about my age, well-groomed and outgoing. A car sales guy. He said he did not remember anyone being with Westonovic, but it had been a busy day for him, he had made three sales, and he might have forgotten. Or, I thought, Billy may have stayed in the background.

As we stood by my car in visitor parking, Hector's eyes scanned the lot like radar, looking for walkup customers. I took the enlarged photos I had of Graham and Billy out of an envelope and showed them to him. He took hold of Billy's photo and his eyes widened, not surprising since it was a mug shot.

"Yeah, that's him. He was kind of edgy, but, hey, it was a cash deal." He pointed at Graham. "But I never saw this guy."

I put Graham's photo back in the envelope and held

up Billy's. "Take another look. Are you sure this is the guy you sold the car to?"

"Oh, yeah. He looked better, but that's Graham Westonovic."

* * *

I called Detective Taylor right away. He answered the phone with, "Okay, Brink, I hope you got something good for me."

I laughed. I told him about Billy Mayfair posing as Graham Westonovic. "The sales guy said he just gets the driver's license number from the customer, who writes it on a form. He doesn't really look at the license photo."

"We got forensics back," Taylor said. "The only clear prints in the car were Billy Mayfair's, which we got from NYPD. The victim's prints were not inside the car."

"Stephanie's note said she wanted to meet with Graham," I said. "Maybe she did, but it wasn't Graham who showed up."

"Does this sales guy know it was the wrong guy?"

"No, I acted like I just wanted to be really sure. He asked why all the questions, I told him I was not at liberty to say, but not to worry, he had done nothing wrong. He was so nervous from seeing the mug shot, he was just glad to get rid of me."

Final Part

"I think I'll wait before talking to the dealership," Taylor said, "and you keep this under your hat, okay. I don't want it to get back to Mayfair that we're looking for him. He's got enough money now to go anywhere."

Chapter 32

earlier in the year

Billy Mayfair noticed that the RV was in real good shape and had California plates. Maybe that was why the dude's accent sounded wrong but familiar; maybe he was new in town, in from the West Coast.

Dude told him to find something good on the radio, which he did. Turned the volume way up. They rode with the windows open, blasting hip-hop.

Dude drove into an industrial district in the Bronx. Parked behind an abandoned warehouse.

"Back in a sec." Dude had a key to the lock on the chain that secured the roll-up garage door next to the loading dock. He opened it, came back, drove inside. They both got out.

Place was cavernous. Sounds echoing. Junk scattered everywhere. Puddles on the concrete floor. Dark,

Final Part

except for feeble light leaking in through grimy, yellowed windows high up on the walls.

Dude had the chain and lock with him. Closed the garage door, locked it from the inside.

Uh-oh.

Dude came up to Billy and pointed a gun at him.

Without hesitation, Billy charged into the dude. Knocked him on his ass. Gun went flying. Billy pounced on it before the dude could react. Fired a shot, hit the dude's foot. And it was all over.

* * *

Sitting on the cold, damp, concrete floor, hogtied and naked, Graham was at Billy's mercy. And Billy Mayfair was merciless.

He kept pouring water on his prisoner, never let him dry. From time to time, he rewarded him with a few of the M&Ms he had found in the RV; otherwise, Graham ate nothing and was given just a little water to drink. On the other hand, Billy ate and slept well. The RV was well stocked and had a most comfortable bed.

Graham's untreated wound stopped bleeding on its own, then swelled, turned blue-black and throbbed unrelentingly. He urinated and defecated where he was. When the odor annoyed Billy, he dragged his prisoner away to a fresh spot; there was no shortage *of space in the warehouse.*

There was also no shortage of interesting tools, iron bars and miscellaneous items Billy could experiment with to torment Graham. And he occasionally used the gun to go after a rat, just to remind Graham that he could turn it on him. At night, while Billy slept in the RV, the curious, ravenous rats kept Graham awake.

Too late, the poor guy discovered that he was not up to playing this part. Graham begged and bargained, but to no avail. Billy had all the time in the world and was unfazed, in fact, was amused by his captive's suffering. It took a couple of days for Billy to squeeze every bit of information he could out of him. Helpless, hopeless, Graham ultimately divulged the entire plan.

* * *

Billy may have been street smart, but he knew he was not smart smart. He thought hard about what to do with what he knew, how to take advantage of the plan Graham and his cousin had hatched to murder his useless parents and get a boatload of money.

A few hours later, he gave up. This needed a much better brain than his. Billy did what he had done whenever he needed sage advice before he had split from California. He called his old school chum and

Final Part

dealer, Junior the genius, who had breezed through high school and college. Junior seemed pleased to hear from him, more so after Billy told him his outlandish story.

As usual, Junior knew exactly what to do. While poor Graham listened on speaker phone—Billy was too jittery to hold the phone to his ear and concentrate—Junior carefully reviewed what Billy had learned from Graham and had him coerce a few more details from his hapless captive. Satisfied that they had wrung the sponge dry, Junior instructed Billy how to shoot and kill Graham.

As directed, Billy shot Graham in the head, wrapped the body in a tarp he found in the warehouse, loaded it into the RV, and dropped it in a dumpster a few blocks away. He tossed the plates from the RV into another dumpster and left the vehicle unlocked, with the keys inside, under an overpass in Harlem.

Junior had told him to toss the gun in the river, but Billy could not resist. He sold it in no time for $750 to a random guy hawking drugs on the street. The dude offered drugs in payment, but Billy took the cash. Junior had been adamant, he had to stay clean and sober for this scam to work. It would be worth it; it would set Billy up for life.

He had Graham's wallet and cell phone. He had a few other items Junior told him to take. He was now Billy Mayfair playing the part of Graham Westonovic playing the part of Billy Mayfair. He had Junior as his script writer and director, and Stephanie Cunningham as his audience.

Act 1, Scene 1: Get a job.

Chapter 33

Our building was owned by a wealthy family that had been in the Valley for over a century. Over time, they had built many of the small commercial buildings that now comprise downtown Campbell, Los Gatos, Willow Glen and Saratoga.

All these properties were managed by Archie Johannsen. Archie was about 60. His blonde hair was thinning and whitening. He was what my mom would describe as 'thick though the waist' and wore a constant air of disappointment at living in a world where things broke.

Archie had a three-pronged approach to dealing with tenant repair issues. Turn emergencies into non-emergencies; fix it himself; delay. In that order.

He would show up at random intervals, unannounced, as he had today, to be sure each tenant knew how to take the emergency out of emergencies. This was done by providing instruction on all the utility shutoffs, gas, electricity and water, that were conveniently located in one cabinet. Archie's opinion was that, if water or gas leaked or the electric circuits were going haywire, the tenant should shut them off. No more emergency. That you no longer had gas, electricity or water was merely an inconvenience. As for sewage problems, well, if the toilet was backing up, stop using it.

Archie did not respond to phone calls. His recorded message reminded the caller that, if there was danger, shut off the offending utility. He also had an abiding belief that PG&E would respond to most dangerous gas and electrical problems, which took them off his plate as emergencies. In this, he was correct.

Now that you no longer had an emergency, you were advised to send an email. He would respond within one business day. Maybe two. Then he would ruthlessly triage the problem. No amount of cajoling could get a commitment as to when it would be fixed. But, eventually, Archie would show up without warning, at his convenience.

When he did come to make a repair, Archie wore a toolbelt sporting an impressive array of screwdrivers, wrenches and hammers. But his real magic was in his van. There he had a cornucopia of tools—including the oft-used and popular snake for clearing pipe clogs—and all manner of miscellaneous parts. On occasion, he did have to go to a hardware store for some part or tool, but he seemed able to fix almost anything. In the event he could not fix it, he would solemnly announce that he was "putting it on the queue." The queue was like a

Final Part

black hole. Once something went in, it never came out. I'd had two items put on the queue. I ended up taking care of them myself. Which, of course, was the idea.

In any event, today was our building's day to be blessed with Archie's presence. He spent ten minutes with me going over the emergency shut off procedures, a completely unnecessary task, as they were so simple. The shutoffs were in a closet at the end of the hall, near the staircase. The closet door opened with the key I kept in my desk. The gadget needed for each valve hung by a wire from said valve. Everything was clearly labelled.

I think the purpose of the exercise was to reinforce the no-emergencies policy.

Archie had already been downstairs. Sally was teaching a class, and he sat in my office stewing over the few minutes he would have to wait before he could speak with her.

"Any idea on who my new neighbor is going to be? What kind of tenant improvements you'll be doing." *How much disruption I'll have to deal with?*

If anything, Archie's expression turned fouler.

"We won't be doing anything for a while."

"How come?"

Archie explained that he and the owners had been delaying seismic retrofitting and handicapped access requirements in our building for years. They had been put on notice: come into compliance in six months or the building would be condemned.

Yikes! "I thought you did the handicapped stuff last year."

"I did the easy stuff." Meaning inexpensive. "Wider doors. New fixtures in the bathrooms. That sort of thing. I was hoping it would buy us a few more years."

"So what now?"

"You ever notice anyone in a wheelchair up here, detective?"

"No, now that you mention it."

"Of course not. How would they get up the stairs?"

Duh!

"We gotta put in an elevator," Archie said. "It'll go in the alley, next to the staircase. Open up in the stairwell. The work will start next month."

"What about the seismic work?"

"I got an engineer we've used in other buildings. Knows compliance." Meaning minimal compliance. "He says we can do it while the elevator work is going on."

As women piled out of Sally's studio, she came to my open door. "Okay, Archie," Sally said, "let's get this nonsense over with."

Chapter 34

It was to be a day of many case theories, a sure sign that a case is getting away from you. Otherwise known as grasping at straws.

"It doesn't look good for Graham Westonovic, does it?" Boomer said, as he walked into my office, helped himself to a soda and plopped himself in a chair. He was coming off the mountain into the Valley a lot more often these days.

"You mean like maybe he's dead too?" I said. "It does appear that Mayfair is cleaning up behind him."

"How do you figure it?"

"We know Stephanie Cunningham knew the Mayfairs. She'd been seeing them for awhile before they died. We know from her note she and Graham were involved in some sort of play, and I had disrupted it with my inquiries. We know she planned to meet Graham. We know Billy Mayfair drove the car she was found dead in."

"The note could have been planted," Boomer said.

"Unlikely. They only found her prints on the note, they compared it to other samples of her writing and it matched, and there was no evidence of anyone else recently being inside her place."

"Okay."

"We know Billy impersonated Graham and bought the car. We know he had Graham's driver's license. So, let's say Billy killed Graham and impersonated him."

"But Billy was in New York when Sharon and Tommy were killed," Boomer said.

"Suppose Graham killed them," I said. "Then Billy came here and killed him."

"So, they knew each other and somehow planned it together?"

I nodded. "I think Graham got the idea from his cousin, who knew this old couple who had a ton of money." I explained stepped-up basis, how the capital gain would not be taxed if the parents died without selling the property.

"But if Graham and Billy already knew each other that well, what are the odds his cousin would just happen to have Billy's parents in her caseload?"

"What if she somehow selected them? At least that's something I can check out." I picked up the phone. It only took one call to County Public Health. Stephanie Cunningham's cases were assigned to her. I told Boomer.

"Maybe it worked the other way," I said. "It starts with Stephanie, she involves Graham, he involves Billy. Stephanie and Graham do the Mayfairs, Billy comes

Final Part

west and cashes in, then bumps off his partners."

"Still quite a coincidence," Boomer said, "Graham knowing Billy, and Stephanie happening to have the Mayfairs in her caseload."

"But it could have been exactly that. Stephanie just happens to have the Mayfairs in her caseload, Graham just happens to know Billy, and opportunity knocks."

"And Suzy Lou was collateral damage," Boomer said.

* * *

Detective Taylor had called and told me I wanted to come see him. The way he said it, I did. We sat in one of the interview rooms to have some privacy.

"We have a new theory of the case," he said.

"Tell me."

"You know Stephanie Cunningham was divorced, right? That she got bupkis, then her ex made a killing on his startup and married a trophy wife? Then the ex and his pregnant new wife were murdered in their bed in a Cancun resort?"

I had not known that. I had not dug that deeply into Stephanie's background. I was going to, but I was up to my eyeballs in the Conrad case. Then she got killed, and I had not yet picked up that thread again.

"We think that was a hit-for-hire, Stephanie's revenge. We think she contracted with a Mexican gang through someone local here. Let's call him Mr. X."

"I assume you have some evidence of that?"

"Nah, we were all just sitting around bullshitting and made up this fairytale. Of course we have evidence."

I knew better than to ask what it was. Sharing went just so far. "Okay, I'm with you."

"Did you ever wonder how Billy Mayfair navigated through all the crap he had to do after his parents died? He was not the brightest bulb on the tree."

That I knew. I had visited Billy's high school and talked to his former homeroom teacher who was now a guidance counselor. She was reluctant to speak to me, but I assured her I only wanted her impression of what sort of a kid Billy was, not any confidential records. She either succumbed to my charm or decided to toss me a bone to get rid of me.

She said Billy was academically challenged, skipped school a lot, and applied little effort when he did show up. When I asked about him dropping out, she said his absences became longer and he sort of drifted away.

"I assume the family lawyer helped him," I said to Taylor. "He was coming into enough money to pay for legal services."

"Yeah, Mr. Attorney-Client Privilege probably did. But you've been looking for Billy, we've been looking for Billy, and he's still in the wind. Billy Mayfair is not that clever."

Taylor was leading me by the nose and enjoying it. I

Final Part

was getting fed up. "You mind getting to the point?"

"We think Stephanie came across the Mayfairs and saw an opportunity. She contacts her local gangster, the guy she dealt with to do her ex and his wife. She tells him about the Mayfairs and her idea to rip them off. She needs help killing the Mayfairs. But it has to look like an accident. For Mr. X, this is a piece of cake. He has resources, they have no problem putting two feeble old folks in their car, into the lake, staging the accident."

"Okay."

"Mr. X takes over. When Billy gets back in town, Mr. X hooks up with him. Becomes his mentor. Coaches him through the legal and financial stuff. Stephanie knows about this; she's going to get her cut. Only you panic her, she contacts Mr. X, he decides she's a liability, plus he prefers to keep her cut. He has Billy kill Stephanie, probably with help. He has them leave Stephanie's body in Billy's car, making sure his guy leaves no prints. Billy, feeling like a big-time hood, does what he's told."

Taylor looked pleased with himself. I had to give him credit, it all hung together.

"Now what does he need Billy for?"

"I'll get to that."

"What about Graham Westonovic?"

"Yes, the elusive Graham," Taylor said. "Who no one has seen since the beginning of the year. Whose credit cards and bank account have been dormant. There's no evidence the man is still alive."

"You think he's dead?"

"We think he's long dead. The last credit card activity puts him in San Jose in January. Then, poof, he's gone. We think Cousin Stephanie had something to do with that. For some reason, she held onto his ID. Maybe part of the plan with Mr. X. We haven't worked that out yet."

"What about the note? Keep close tabs on G. Meet with G."

Taylor smiled the smile of a man about to make a great revelation. At least he didn't say ta-da. "We think Mr. X is actually Señor G. We've got no shortage of capable gangsters in the area with Mexican ties whose names begin with G. Garcia, Gonzalez, Gomez, and so forth. Too many to count. Or it could be the first name, like Guillermo or Geraldo. Whatever."

"What about Suzy Lou?"

"We think Billy screwed up and told her something he shouldn't have. Or, like you say, maybe it had something to do with the car. Whatever, she had to be silenced. We have Stephanie's flights to Maui on either side of the so-called accident, her credit card record for her hotel, car rental, and so forth. We think she met one of Señor G's guys there."

"What now?"

"Now, we need to smoke out Señor G."

Final Part

"Let's assume you're right," I said. "As far as Señor G is concerned, he's in the clear. We're all focused on finding Graham and Billy."

"But we haven't made that public yet," Taylor said. "I mean, Graham's been identified as the car's owner, but nothing about Billy is out there."

"Because you didn't want to spook Billy."

"Right."

"You got a plan?" I said.

"I thought you'd never ask."

Chapter 35

Detective Taylor and Detective Nguyen were concerned that, if he had not already done so, Señor G might soon eliminate Billy Mayfair. We needed to give him a reason to keep Billy alive. We also needed a way to catch the elusive young man.

My role was to convince Indira Kapoor to go along with the little ploy we had cooked up. Time was critical, so I got right on the phone as soon as I got back to my office.

"I hope you've got good news for me," she said by way of greeting.

I told her the plan. She did not seem to think it was the good news she yearned for.

"I don't like it, but, I hate to say, it actually makes sense."

"Is that a yes?"

"That's an, 'I'll pitch it to my boss.'"

Indira must have gotten the urgency, because she called me back in less than 30 minutes. "We'll do it on two conditions. One, we deal with the cops, not you; you're working for us and have to stay out of it. Two,

Final Part

we got a stack of waivers they'll need to sign, us being an insurance company and all."

I called Detective Taylor. He answered on the third ring.

* * *

The email went out from the insurance company to Billy Mayfair, hard copy mailed to his family attorney, that afternoon. It said that they had reviewed his appeal of their decision to delay paying on his parents' policies pending completion of their investigation, and were happy to inform him that payment on all three policies had been approved, for a total of $750,000.

It went on to say that, per company policy, a check for this amount had to be picked up and signed for by the payee in person, and gave him a name and number to call to arrange for that to occur. Which was bullshit.

The trap was set.

* * *

Billy Mayfair's body was discovered a few days later by the maid in a room in a "don't ask, don't tell" motel in a seedy section of Oakland. The needle that sent the heroin overdose into his body was still in his arm.

He was fully clothed, on the bed, on top of the shabby spread. Except for his wallet, which contained about $2,000 in cash, no other belongings were found. In particular, no phone.

The room was registered to John Smith. Cash had been paid. No one remembered seeing anything. The clerk who had been on duty at reception did not remember Billy. The place had no working security cameras. No useful evidence was found.

It was, the cops concluded, just another in the unending flow of drug overdose deaths.

Billy Mayfair had never responded to the insurance company.

* * *

"Were back to looking for Graham Westonovic." Even over the phone, I could sense the frustration in Detective Nicki Nguyen's voice.

"What about Señor G?"

"Yeah, about that. Completely unrelated to this case, San Jose had an undercover agent who heard about a guy known among some of our less seemly citizens as Señor G. The undercover cop was getting close to him. His intel is what gave us the Señor G idea."

"That was your evidence?"

"I know it was thin, but we were grasping."

Talk about Boomer and me making up fairy tales. "So what happened?"

Final Part

"San Jose just arrested the mutt. His name is Gonzolo Leon. He's a broker, hooks up people here with bad guys in Mexico. You want someone roughed up or maybe killed there? Got a relative you need brought into the States? Whatever, Gonzolo will broker the transaction. He's got connections everywhere down there."

"So?"

"Gonzolo is now dealing like crazy to save his ass. He's got a lot of good stuff to trade. The U.S. Attorney has taken over and the Mexican Federales sent a guy up, the information is so good. It's real clear Gonzolo Leon isn't our mastermind. He brokered the Cancun killings for Stephanie Cunningham alright, but that was it."

"You're sure?"

"You know how it works. He coughs up information, his sentence is reduced. Repeat. But if anything turns out to be a lie, the entire deal goes away. I can't give you chapter and verse, but, yeah, we're sure."

"What now?"

"We're trying to track the money," she said.

"You think Graham's got it?"

"It's what this whole sorry mess was all about. With Stephanie Cunningham and Billy Mayfair dead, he's the last crook standing."

"He's also probably their murderer," I said. *And damn good at hiding out.*

"Maybe. Or maybe Billy did Stephanie for some reason and Graham did Billy in revenge. Or Billy may have just been an OD."

"We still don't really know much, do we?"

"We know plenty, Joe," Detective Nguyen said. "Just not enough."

"So, the money?"

"It seems it's been sliced and diced and wired all over the world. Detective Taylor is trying to get the FBI to help; they're good at this stuff. It isn't exactly a priority for them, but it's all we have. Everything else has turned into a dead-end."

I knew a bigshot at the FBI from a previous case. I thought maybe I could get him interested and speed things up. I really wanted closure for Boomer, but it would have to wait. I had Sally's advanced class to start. And a trial to prepare for.

I also felt a load of guilt about Billy Mayfair's death. Our little scheme, intended to keep Billy alive and snare him, had backfired. I did not for a minute believe that Billy had overdosed. Whoever was orchestrating him had decided Billy had outlived his usefulness and, I felt certain, had somehow seen through our trap.

Chapter 36

"Joe, wake up."

Climbing out of the fog, I felt Anna hand shaking my shoulder. "What's wrong?"

"Listen!"

I could have sworn I heard "Go, Diego, go!" It was coming from the living room. *What the...*

Brave PI that I was, I got out of bed, turned on the light and shouted, "I've got a gun. I'm calling 9-1-1 now."

Knowing I had no gun, Anna looked at me quizzically and reached for the phone. I shook my head no and put my finger on my lips to keep her quiet.

I slowly poked my head out the door. I could see light flashing in the living room and heard Diego's high-pitched voice. I flipped on the light, expecting to confront intruders. Instead, I saw Diego and his cartoon buddies on an animal rescue mission on my living room TV.

A few minutes later, I had cleared the other rooms and confirmed that the front door was still locked and the security system set.

Phil Bookman

It was 3 a.m. I told Anna I'd figure out what went wrong with the TV in the morning and we went back to bed.

* * *

I went for my morning run, bewildered by the previous night's TV escapade. When I got back, Anna had already left for work. I, who made my own hours, fixed pancakes for breakfast and read the morning paper.

Pancakes done, I was starting to clean up when the TV came on. It displayed a weird black and white picture with a voice-over saying:

"There is nothing wrong with your television set. Do not attempt to adjust the picture. We are controlling transmission. If we wish to make it louder, we will bring up the volume. If we wish to make it softer, we will tune it to a whisper. We will control the horizontal. We will control the vertical. We can roll the image, make it flutter. We can change the focus to a soft blur or sharpen it to crystal clarity..."

The TV shut off and there was a knock on my door. I opened it. Jonathan and Charles were standing there with big, goofy grins.

"Welcome to the *Outer Limits*," Charles said. Then they both cracked up.

* * *

Final Part

We all sat down. After a segue to explain that I had been treated to the introduction to the original *Outer Limits*, a TV show from the 1960s I had never heard of, my neighbors explained the strange goings on with my new TV.

I knew Jonathan and Charles worked with computers, but in Silicon Valley that was akin to saying they breathed air. We had never talked about exactly what kind of work they did because I usually get lost about two sentences into such conversations.

The guys were what is known as white-hat hackers. "It means we use our powers for good, not evil," Charles intoned, doing a James Earl Jones imitation.

They were consultants and worked for companies who hired them to test the security of their systems. They would try to hack in and, if successful, which they usually were, report the vulnerabilities to the company and, often, tell them how to fix them.

"Who are your customers?"

"You name a big company, they're a potential client," Jonathan said. "Today, every big company depends on its IT. And we have great job security. The bad guys keep finding new ways to break in, and corporate IT is always playing catchup."

"What's this have to do with my TV?"

"We also try to hack tech products for bounties." He said that tech companies would pay hackers who found a vulnerability in their product, so they could quietly fix it before it became public.

"We were using you as a guinea pig." Charles said. "We've figured out a way to combine an exploit of your smart TV with an exploit of your cable box. We can take control of your TV and cable box remotely. Remember when we came over and I asked you for your Wi-Fi password for my phone? I also used it to access your Wi-Fi from our condo on my iPad. Then I side-loaded an app onto the TV and used that as my point of entry."

I had no idea what side-loaded meant, not an unusual feeling for me when techies talk tech.

"Now we can take complete control from anywhere, better than you can with the remote. We can push down content, like that *Outer Limits* intro. We can even listen in."

"I may not be a computer whiz," I said, "but I know the TV doesn't have a microphone."

"I've got a gun. I'm calling 9-1-1 now," Charles intoned seriously.

I was taken aback, then remembered it was what I had said to try to scare off the non-existent intruder.

Charles picked up the remote and pointed at it. "This has a microphone right here. You use it to give voice commands to the DVR."

"But I have to press the button so it'll listen."

"The hardware and software already support voice

Final Part

activation, like Alexa. The cable company just isn't using that capability yet. We start it listening through code."

We had gotten about as deep into the technology as I could go without becoming hopelessly lost. "Okay, I sort of get it. It was a good prank."

"The thing is," Jonathan said, "being able to listen in on people is a huge privacy issue, but the public doesn't seem to realize how big yet. When they do, the shit will really hit the fan."

They went on to tell me that the hard part was going to be getting the TV manufacturer and cable company to pay attention to the security problems they had discovered. It seems the smart TV manufacturers were new to internet security issues and still didn't quite get it. And the cable company was notoriously combative and defensive.

Before the guys left, they had me change my Wi-Fi password and showed me how to safely set up a separate account for guests. I could now give out the guest account without compromising the security of my devices. They also put everything back the way it was before they had hacked in. Or so they said. How was I to know for sure?

Chapter 37

"The theme of self-defense is escape and survive. That's always the best alternative. But when that's not possible, it's time for offense. The theme for offense is fast and furious."

My arm had healed, and it was time to begin Sally Rocket's intensive, one-on-one, advanced class. I stood barefoot on the mat-covered floor in Sally's studio, in shorts and a T-shirt. Sally, similarly clad, faced me. She was all business.

"I'm going to teach you how to use your head, hands, arms, legs and feet as weapons. I'm going to drill you until muscle memory makes your moves automatic. You will never be as sore and worn out as you'll be at the end of our sessions."

I wondered if Sally had been in the military. She would have been a fine drill instructor for basic training.

"When you go on offense, you attack without hesitation and without mercy. You will learn to move more quickly than you ever imagined possible. Most fights are over in seconds, not minutes. You need to own the

Final Part

action during those seconds."

So we began. Every weekday morning from 7 to 8. Sally was right. I was aching and exhausted after each session.

On those days, I ate a light breakfast before coming to the studio. Afterwards, I packed in the carbs at the pancake house down the block.

I learned to use my legs a lot. Sally said most guys do not expect you to use your legs and are unprepared for that. I learned to use my opponent's moves and momentum to gain leverage and add power to my punches and kicks. And I learned how to protect my head in the process. The doctor had warned me about any more concussions. I did not want to end up like so many NFL players.

Speaking of the NFL, after a couple of weeks, Bubba joined our sessions. Bubba, whose real name was Lester Payne, had played lineman on the practice squads of both the Raiders and 49ers.

"I never was quite fast enough or big enough to make the big show," he told me.

He was sure big and fast enough for me. I'm six feet tall, 180 on a heavy day. Bubba towered over me and had to weigh over 250 pounds but moved with a quickness I could not match.

"Time for you to have someone else to practice with," Sally said. "This way, I can watch and coach."

It was a good idea. Size-wise, Bubba was in the same

class as the Bigs who had put me in the hospital, except substituting muscle for fat. He was also quick and gave new meaning to the phrase "as strong as an ox."

Practicing with Bubba not only left me beat, it left me beat up. But my skills grew. My body hardened. Sally gave me specific instructions for my workouts at the gym.

One day, after a particularly satisfying session, I told Bubba I was getting tougher. Bubba, who had become a high school PE teacher and coach after it became clear that his NFL career wasn't going to happen, said, "Toughness is the ability to take punishment. Skill is the ability to avoid taking punishment. You're becoming more skillful. Tough is a by-product."

I figured Bubba's students were in good hands.

Chapter 38

The trial of Timothy Conrad for the manslaughter of Ruby Swanson had begun.

After her opening statement—Dell chose to reserve his opening until he began the defense case—the prosecutor, Assistant District Attorney Myrna Thatcher, quickly established the foundation of the case with the testimony of the responding detective and medical examiner, who together established the timeframe and cause of death. The ME said the blow was most likely struck left-handed, probably with a large crescent wrench. The detective said that a witness named Janice Sheltenham had picked Ruby out of a photo array and Tim out of a lineup. He also testified as to the make, model and color of Ruby's car.

Three witnesses were called who placed Ruby and Tim together in the bar. The cocktail waitress testified about them being in a rush to leave, and Tim's credit card charge that confirmed the date and time was introduced into evidence. Each of the couple who found Ruby's body testified to that effect.

One of Tim's employees reluctantly testified that

Tim was indeed left-handed, drove a truck, and kept tools in it.

Dell made few objections and his cross-examinations were perfunctory. He did get the detective to admit that no weapon had been found and there was no physical evidence linking Tim to the actual crime. He asked each of the bar witnesses what the demeanor of the couple had been. They either did not recall or said they seemed to be getting along just fine. And he got Tim's employee to agree that he had no idea if Tim had driven his truck to Widow O'Toole's that night.

On day two, Myrna Thatcher closed her case with her big gun, Janice Sheltenham. She kept it short and sweet. Janice stuck to her deposition. She testified that she had left Dominici's a little after 11 p.m. As she was getting into her car, she saw a woman in the next-door parking lot running. A man was right behind her. He was yelling, and, though she could not recall the exact words, she was sure he had called her a cockteaser. He caught her next to a dark colored car and spun her around, shouting obscenities. He seemed to be holding something in his left hand, though she could not see what it was.

Janice was shown a photograph of Ruby taken a few weeks before her death and confirmed she was the woman. When asked if the man was in the courtroom, she pointed at Tim. It was a classic courtroom moment.

On cross, Dell poked around at Janice's testimony

Final Part

but landed no serious blows. He asked why she hadn't done something to break up the fight. She said she was not the sort of person to stick her nose into other people's business. She thought it was just another tiff between two people who'd had too much to drink. Asked if she regretted that decision, she said she now did.

Dell got her to reiterate that she had not seen the weapon. Nor had she seen any blows struck. He asked why it had taken her so long to come forward. She repeated her depo testimony almost verbatim. She did not read the newspaper, did not watch local newscasts, and only heard about the death in the parking lot when she returned to Dominici's a week later. She then contacted the police.

"I'm finished with this witness, your honor," Dell said. "But I reserve the right to recall her during the defense case."

"So noted," the judge said. Then we broke for lunch.

* * *

The prosecution had completed their case-in-chief. It was time for Dell to give his opening statement, the one he had deferred at the start of the trial.

"Ruby Swanson met Tim Conrad for the first time at Widow O'Toole's on a Friday night. They hit it off, enjoyed each other's company and left together. You will hear testimony that Ruby had to get home for her sitter by 11:30, and Tim had to pick up his kids at his ex-wife's at 8 a.m. the next morning. So, they left promptly at 11 p.m. and went to their separate vehicles to go home.

"Perhaps Tim should have waited to see Ruby drive off, but he didn't. Widow O'Toole's is a nice place, in a relatively crime-free neighborhood, and the well-lit parking lot seemed safe enough. It was a mistake.

"There is no physical evidence tying Tim Conrad to the assault that took her life, because he was already on his way home when it occurred. There is a witness, but we ask you to wait for us to present our case before you evaluate her testimony.

"Someone accosted Ruby before she could get into her car and leave that night. Someone killed her. But it was not Tim Conrad."

I thought it was a good opening, simple and straightforward. Dell implied he would discredit Janice Sheltenham's testimony. What he did not say, but what I knew, is that he would top that by revealing the real killer.

Chapter 39

"The defense recalls Janice Sheltenham."

As the witness was reminded that she was still under oath, I gave Anna's hand a squeeze. She had taken the day off to join me in court, in part because what was coming next had been her idea.

"Mrs. Sheltenham, Dominici's is a bit out of the way for you, is it not?"

"It is. It's also expensive. I only shop there when I'm planning to fix something special."

"Is that why you were there that night?"

"Yes. It was the anniversary of the day my husband proposed, and I was planning a special dinner for him."

That had been a hole in her deposition story that Anna had picked up, the why. It seemed likely that the prosecutor had realized that and Janice had come up with an answer, one that would be hard to disprove.

Dell cast a skeptical glance at the jury. Then asked, "What did you make for that dinner?"

Janice looked startled, then confused. "I don't understand…"

"It's really a simple question. What gourmet dish did

you prepare for this most special occasion?"

"That was months ago. I know it was something French. Let me think."

Dell looked again at the jury. He shook his head. "Perhaps it was Coq Au Vin? Boeuf Bourguignon? Cassolette? Maybe Bouillabaisse or Ratatouille?"

"Objection! Counsel is badgering the witness."

"Sustained. But the witness will answer the question."

"What was the question?" Janice said.

The judge signaled the court reporter, who read, "What gourmet dish did you prepare for this most special occasion?"

"I just don't remember."

"Perhaps you remember the ingredients? The ones you went miles out of your way to purchase at an expensive, gourmet market?"

She shook her head.

"Please answer verbally so the jury can hear you," the judge said.

"I don't remember."

"What wine did you pair with this fine meal?"

"Objection!"

"Sustained. Move on, counselor. You've made your point."

Here I was, the professional investigator, trained to ferret out conflicting details. But this line of inquiry had never occurred to me. It had been the second thing

Final Part

Anna suggested, after the why question. What exactly had she cooked? What was the recipe? What was the wine?

"What do you do for a living?"

Clearly happy to be on firmer ground, Janice replied, "Like I said yesterday, I'm a nurse. I work the graveyard shift at the hospital. The killing occurred on my night off."

"You work around drugs?"

"Of course. It's a hospital."

"Where does your husband work?"

"At the Fremont auto plant. He's also on the graveyard shift. We take the same days off."

"You have two children in college and a third in high school, is that correct?"

"Yes."

"College is sure expensive."

"You're telling me."

"Must put a strain on your budget."

The prosecutor rose. "Your honor, I object. Relevance?"

"If you'll give me just a few more questions," Dell said, "I think the court will be satisfied as to relevance."

"Go ahead, counselor, but get there fast."

"Did you have HVAC repairs in your house a few months ago?"

"Yes."

"Did Kevin Hill do the work?"

"Objection! Your honor, aren't we getting far afield?"

"Overruled. Please answer the question."

"I don't recall the man's name."

"Your honor, I'd like to place a copy of the receipt we obtained from Mr. Hill's employer into evidence." Dell handed a copy to the prosecutor.

"No objection."

The receipt was logged into evidence, then Dell showed it to Janice. "Is that your name and address?"

"Yes."

"Do you see where it has the technician's name? What does it say?"

Janice looked pleadingly at Myrna Thatcher, who remained stone-faced. "Kevin Hill."

"Your honor, I can call a witness to verify that Kevin Hill is Ruby Swanson's ex-husband. But perhaps Ms. Thatcher would be willing to stipulate to that to save us all some time?"

The judge looked at the prosecutor. "So stipulated," she said.

"Tie it up, counselor," the judge said to Dell.

"Mrs. Sheltenham, isn't it true that you have been stealing medication from the hospital and giving it to your husband to sell to coworkers at the plant? And isn't it true that Kevin Hill somehow became aware of that when he worked at your home?"

A buzz swept through the gallery. Thatcher shouted,

Final Part

"Objection!" Simultaneously, Janice Sheltenham said, "No, no, it isn't true."

Before the judge could respond to the objection, Dell raised his voice above the uproar. "Isn't it true that Mr. Hill threatened to expose both of you if you didn't make up a story that you saw Tim Conrad kill his ex-wife?"

"Your honor!" Thatcher shouted.

"Mr. Chamberlin!" shouted the judge.

In a normal tone, Dell said, "My apologies, your honor. I have no more questions for this witness." He shook his head and turned in the direction of the jury, disgust plainly visible on his face, and took his seat at the defense table.

"The jury will ignore the last two questions," the judge said. As if, as they say in the legal profession, you could unring a bell. He asked Myrna Thatcher, "Any cross?"

The prosecutor was in a quandary. She needed to rehabilitate her star witness. At the same time, she did not want to expose her to a subsequent redirect, for fear Dell might come up with a clever way to inflict even more damage.

"Nothing, your honor."

"The defense calls Cora Corcoran."

Chapter 40

While I was in the hospital recovering from the beating at Baldy's, I had got to thinking about Janice Sheltenham's lame excuse for not having a receipt for her groceries.

Dell had already subpoenaed her credit card and bank statements. Sure enough, the Sheltenhams used checks only to pay bills, like the mortgage, utilities and the kids' college expenses. Credit cards were for hotels, airline tickets, the occasional online purchase, and little else.

In my hospital room, I thought, *Who lives that way?* People who want to leave no paper trail of their expenses, and, more importantly, who have significant undeclared cash income. As in drug dealers.

The rest was investigative legwork. After I had healed for a few days, I hung out around Janice's hospital for a week, before and after the night shift, buttonholing workers as they went on and off duty. I'm sure it got back to Janice that this PI was asking about her, but I didn't care. She already knew she was under Tim's defense team's microscope. I spoke to several

Final Part

people who had worked with Janice. Mostly, they had nothing bad to say about her, nothing that helped me. But then there was nurse Olga, assistant head nurse on Janice's ward, geriatrics.

After her shift, over coffee at Starbucks, Olga unloaded. Her gripe was that Janice gave her patients, who should have been sleeping, too much PRN painkiller medication. Olga thought Janice was too softhearted. Janice claimed she could tell that the poor dears were suffering. Olga said if Janice just left them alone instead of waking them, they would be fine. She objected to giving them opioids unless absolutely necessary and lectured me about the opioid epidemic. She thought the doctors who said these were old people and they deserved to live their remaining time without pain were wrong-headed. She also wanted Janice spending more time at the nursing station completing paperwork and electronic chart entries.

It did not take professional detective training to imagine that it would be easy for kindly Nurse Janice to cadge opioid tablets. Considering their street value, even a few each shift could be quite lucrative.

How, I wondered, would Janice sell the purloined pills? Following a hunch, I hung around the bus stop outside the Fremont auto plant gate. A bus stop is a good place to meet people who are chronically in need of money. I paid a night janitor $250 to nose around for dirt on Janice's husband. I promised another

$1,000 if he got useful information but gave him no clue as to what I was looking for. We also had a heart-to-heart about not trying to feed me bullshit.

Ricardo came through. Word in the plant was that, if you wanted opioids, Rod Sheltenham was the guy to see.

* * *

I had been proud of my great detecting, uncovering the Sheltenham drug ring. Sitting in his soon-to-be demolished office, Dell was pleased, but not ready to break out the champagne.

"That'll help me cast doubt on her honesty, and it may be enough, but it doesn't explain why she would lie about that night. Jurors want to know that."

Which brought me back to investigating Kevin Hill. This time, I was determined to avoid his band of big guys.

Briana Brisco, Ruby Swanson's best friend, had given me the lowdown on Kevin's drunken rages. The beatdown at Baldy's had given me the sense that he did not want anyone nosing around his alibi, that he had been with Cora Corcoran and could not have gotten to Widow O'Toole's in time to kill Ruby.

I met with Sarge, who had become pals with Boomer, at the fro-yo shop. I bought him a large cone and told him what I was really doing at Baldy's that

Final Part

night, enough to get him to tell me that Kevin did not return until near midnight the night of the murder. He remembered, he said, because, when Kevin came in he looked agitated and soon word got around that, if anyone asked, good old Kevin had come back with Cora at around 11 o'clock.

Dell had said what we needed was the nexus between Kevin Hill and the Sheltenhams. I thought I needed the connection, but, after looking it up, I liked nexus.

I went nuts nexus hunting. Try though I did, I could not find it. They seemingly had nothing in common. I was exasperated and tired of calling and buttonholing people who acted like I was an annoying putz asking stupid questions, when a brain cell that must have still been healing from the concussion came back online. I made a quick check. Yes!

The Sheltenhams had nearly $1,000 of HVAC repair work done on their home a few months ago. They had paid by credit card.

Gotcha!

* * *

Nexus secured, the rest was conjecture. Dell said it did not have to be exactly right, just enough right to fluster Janice Sheltenham, make her look like she was a perjuring crook, and tee-up Kevin Hill.

Phil Bookman

Dell was ready for his Perry Mason moment. He was about to expose the real killer in person in open court.

Chapter 41

I left the courtroom. Cora Corcoran was sitting on a bench in the hallway with Sally, who was acting as her babysitter. Cora could have left at any time, but Sally was doing her ghetto intimidation thing and I don't think Cora wanted to test her.

Kevin Hill was seated on another bench about ten feet away. He was glaring at Cora. Cora was looking at her hands, which were folded in her lap.

Sally and I escorted Cora into the courtroom.

After she was sworn in, Dell established where Cora worked and that she knew Kevin Hill. Then, that she was working the night Ruby Swanson was killed and that Kevin was in the bar.

"On that night, did you spend some time in your van with Mr. Hill?"

"Yes."

"What time might that have been?"

"It was at 10:30, when I take my break."

"How long was Mr. Hill in your van with you?"

"About five minutes."

"What did you two do during those five minutes?"

"We started to, you know, get ready for sex. Then he got a text. I think it was a photo. Anyway, he got pissed and said he had to go take care of something. Then he left."

"When did you see him next?"

"I'm not sure exactly. He got back to the bar around midnight or so."

"That same night?"

"Yes."

"And did Mr. Hill say anything to you when he returned to the bar around midnight?"

"We stepped out back behind the building to be alone. Kevin said that if anyone asked, he needed me to say he was with me until eleven o'clock and we came right back into the bar together."

"Did anyone ask?"

"Yes, the police came around asking questions a couple of days later."

"Did you tell the police the story Mr. Hill had asked you to?"

"Yes."

"Did Mr. Hill say why he wanted you to lie?"

"No."

"Tell us, Cora, why did you lie for him?"

"He threatened to have his buddies harm my daughter if I didn't."

"What did you take that to mean?"

Cora began to weep. "I was afraid they would rape

Final Part

her or worse. She's only 14."

"Do you need a short break?" the judge asked Cora,

She sniffled. Dell made a show of handing her his pristine, neatly folded handkerchief. She took it, wiped her eyes, softly blew her nose, and shook her head. "No thank you, I'm okay. I just want to finish this."

"One last question, Cora," Dell said. "Why are you telling the truth today?"

"Because you told me I would go to jail if I lied on the witness stand."

"No further questions, your honor."

Myrna Thatcher asked a few desultory questions on cross, but it was obvious she was just going through the motions. Cora stepped down and sat next to Sally in the gallery. Probably for protection.

"The defense calls Kevin Hill."

* * *

I went out to get Kevin, but he was nowhere to be found. I even checked the men's room. When I got back inside, I noticed that Big, who had been sitting in the aisle seat in the last row, was no longer there. I signaled to Dell by shaking my head, shrugging, and putting both hands palm up, arms extended to the side.

"Counselor?"

"It appears that Mr. Hill has left the courthouse. He was out in the hallway earlier."

"Will you be able to produce your witness?"

"I think it's obvious that this was a hostile witness, your honor," Dell said.

"That, counselor, would be the understatement of the year, if not the century."

I thought the judge was getting a bit grandiose, but it was his courtroom, he ruled supreme, and he had helped make our point in front of the jury.

"I'm going to adjourn until tomorrow morning and issue a bench warrant for Kevin Hill. Let's see if the police can round him up for us."

It was, Dell later told us, an unusual step for the judge to take, but it was good for our client. The jury had heard it all. Clearly the judge thought Kevin Hill was guilty of something and had done a runner. It would not be much of a leap to conclude that the something was the murder of his ex-wife. It was flight as a sign of guilt.

When Hill had not been found by noon the next day, Dell made a motion to dismiss. Myrna Thatcher did not object. Tim Conrad was a free man.

* * *

While the courtroom emptied, Dell and Tim shook hands, and Tim left surrounded by what I assumed were family members.

I looked around the nearly deserted courtroom. It

Final Part

felt like an empty stadium after a championship game. It was hard to imagine that it had just been filled with people engaged in something so dramatic.

Sally had left to take Cora Corcoran home. Cora and her daughter were packing up to move in with her parents in Fresno.

Dell came up to me. "Nice work, Joe. You know, until you put all the pieces together, I really thought our guy was guilty."

We shook hands and walked out together. We had done a great job for Tim Conrad. Dell was a damn good defense attorney. We were a great team. I thought that it was a shame. It would be the last time we worked together. But Dell didn't know that yet.

Chapter 42

"Detective Taylor? Joe Brink. Yeah, I know, its been a while, but I've cracked the Mayfair murders...Yeah, Cunningham and Lou, too...Nah, you'll never guess. Let's just say it's someone I've been real close to recently...Nope, never on your radar...I know, and that's a good word you got there, enigmatic. All will be revealed when I see you. Can you come by tomorrow? I've got some things to wrap up here first thing in the morning, but any time after 11 will work."

* * *

He had been thinking that this ritual was no longer necessary, but he had one more move to make and he needed to know how well it worked. Then it would be time to figure out how to get the recorder out of there.

He listened to yesterday's recordings and blanched. He checked his Rolex. It was a few minutes before 9 a.m. He had no time to call anyone; he had to take care of this himself. He had to move now. Racing out of his office, he told his secretary to clear his calendar, he had

Final Part

a client emergency to deal with.

Twenty-five minutes later, Dell Chamberlin walked into Joe Brink's office, closed the door behind him, and locked the dead bolt.

* * *

"Dell, what brings you here?" I said, painting my face with anxious surprise.

"I think you know why I'm here, Joe."

"I'm afraid I do. You were the brains behind the Mayfair murders. All three of them. Stephanie Cunningham and Suzy Lou, too."

He took a gun out of his pocket and pointed it at me. "Just keep your hands where I can see them."

I put my hands on my desk and switched my look to terrified. Staring at the business end of a gun aimed at me made that easy.

"The Mayfairs were Stephanie's doing," Dell said. "I gotta say, she did a good job staging that accident. She did Suzy Lou, too, though I'll admit we nudged her along with that flashy car thing. It was supposed to reinforce that she was still dealing with her Hollywood wannabe cousin. Your sketch artist idea could have messed that up. The picture might have gone public."

I went for confused, not hard to do, because I was.

Dell laughed. "You still don't get it, do you? The whole thing was Stephanie's idea. She targeted the

Mayfairs. Then she sent her actor cousin to New York to get rid of Billy and replace him. Billy turned the tables on poor Graham. Then he called his old buddy Junior, and we turned the tables on Stephanie. She never even knew about me. She thought Billy was Graham."

"Junior?"

"My child hood nickname. Wardell Chamberlin, Jr. I didn't think the junior part had the dignity I needed as a lawyer, so I dropped it."

"So Graham's dead?"

"Rotting in a dump in New York. Billy was good at taking direction."

"What about Billy?"

"Yeah, well, there was no way to get my hands on that three-quarters of a million. I heard you planning the trap and decided it was time to wrap things up. A dead Billy Mayfair would leave the cops chasing the elusive Graham."

"A lot of murders," I said.

Dell shrugged. "Blame Stephanie Cunningham. I just redirected the money. Billy killed both the cousins."

"You killed Billy."

"Okay, you got me there. Tell me, how did you figure it out?"

"It was when you gave me the Conrad case. You asked if I had enough time to devote to it, what with my

Final Part

insurance case still active. Later, I got to thinking that when I told you about the case the first time we met, it wasn't an insurance case yet. So how, I wondered, did you know it had become an insurance case?"

It was Dell's turn to look confused. "You've been on to me since then?"

"No. It wasn't until I found this." I moved a large envelope that had been covering the device on my desk. "Then I remembered the maintenance guy who came by to work in the ceiling after Mr. Vu left. I checked; the property manager hadn't hired anyone to do any work next door that day. It explained a lot of things, like how you stayed a step ahead of me and why Billy never picked up his insurance check. The business about you knowing it was an insurance case when you shouldn't have just sort of popped out of my memory. Then all the pieces fell into place."

"You are a clever one, Joe. Too bad we won't be working together, we could have done great things. But now it's time for us to go."

He motioned with the gun for me to stand up. As I did, my hand dropped under the edge of my desk for an instant.

CLANG-CLANG-CLANG. YOUR PHOTO HAS BEEN TRANSMITTED TO THE POLICE. THE POLICE ARE ON THEIR WAY. CLANG-CLANG-CLANG.

The noise of my deafening alarm, which I had activated with the panic button under the front edge of my desk, drowned out the sound of the key opening the deadbolt on my door from the outside. The alarm kept repeating. A cop wearing a protective vest came out of my bathroom pointing a gun at Dell. Another came through the front door. They were both screaming for him to drop his weapon and get down on the floor. I fell behind my desk, safely out of the line of fire, and shut off the alarm.

"You can stand up now, Mr. Accidental Hero." I did. Detective Nicki Nguyen was grinning at me. Detective Bart Taylor was placing the bug that had been in my ceiling in an evidence bag. "Hell of an alarm you got there," he said.

The cops had cuffed Dell Chamberlin, who was lying on his stomach on the floor. "You set me up, you fucker," he screamed.

It was my turn to shrug. *Hoisted on you own petard.* The cops had recorded our conversation using his own device. They had his confession.

And Dell's last check for the work I had done on the Conrad case had already cleared.

Chapter 43

After he cussed me out, Dell clammed up and stayed that way. He was charged with multiple counts of murder and murder for financial gain. That meant special circumstances, as in the death penalty. Bail was out of the question. Detective Nguyen and Detective Taylor agreed the case was a slam-dunk.

***

Later that day, a seemingly abandoned carry-on bag created a security scare in Terminal A at San Jose International Airport. Police cordoned off the area as airport personnel herded everyone else out onto the sidewalk.

Three hours later, after the bomb squad had done their thing, the all-clear was sounded. The errant bag contained some underwear, toiletries, and a wallet belonging to a Graham Westonovic. DNA obtained from the toothbrush and hairbrush was later compared to the DNA taken during the autopsy of Stephanie Cunningham. The lab put the likelihood of the two samples coming from first cousins at over 95%.

The police concluded Dell had put this in motion before his arrest, though who he had paid to leave the bag there was never determined. Had Dell not been in custody with a recorded confession, they would have assumed Graham was the mastermind behind all the Mayfair-related murders and had somehow boarded a plane under another identity. He and the five million dollars would have been in the wind, while Dell chortled at their wild-goose chase.

* * *

The same day Dell Chamberlin was arrested, the border patrol apprehended Kevin Hill as he attempted to cross into Mexico. Once Tim Conrad had been acquitted, I was completely off that case, but the police had all the investigative information I had gathered, and Hill was facing multiple felony charges for murdering his ex-wife and coercing Cora Corcoran and Janice Sheltenham to give false information to the authorities.

* * *

When Billy Mayfair was found dead, the insurance company had immediately closed their case. They did not think anyone was going to come after the payment on those policies; they were right.

Final Part

I was then off the Mayfair case and the cops had put it on the back-burner. It still bugged Boomer and me. But, as Dell had planned, I had been buried under by the Conrad case.

It was Jonathan and Charles who gave me the key to uncovering Dell's chicanery when they pulled that stunt with my TV and showed how they could listen in using my remote. That got me thinking that if someone had planted a bug in my office, it would account for a lot of things that had been bothering me in the back of my mind. I remembered the maintenance guy, which led to me getting on a ladder with a flashlight and poking my head up into the area above the suspended ceiling. And there the device was. Listening.

The gadget was spliced into a power line so its battery stayed charged. It was voice activated and recorded only when it picked up voices in the microphone's range, meaning in my office. The flash drive could fill up, so, in the middle of the night, it logged onto the bakery's free Wi-Fi and uploaded the recordings to the cloud. Then it emptied the drive.

I checked with property manager Archie Johannsen, who assured me that no work had been or would be done next door until the seismic retrofit and elevator were completed. No sense spending money until you had to, he said.

I left the gadget in place while I assembled the other

puzzle pieces. Remembering Dell's *faux pas* about calling the Mayfair case an insurance case, when there was no way he should have known that, got me thinking. How he first showed up just as I was getting into the case. How he kept close tabs on my progress on the Conrad case, then backed off about the time of Billy's death. I did some more research on Dell and discovered he had attended the same high school as Billy, just two years ahead.

I met with my friendly detective duo, Taylor and Nguyen, and we hatched the plan to snare Dell. My carefully scripted call to Taylor in the late afternoon with the device left in place was the bait. As I had guessed, Dell habitually listened to the recordings downloaded the night before first thing each morning. After that, it was just a matter of reeling him in.

But Dell Chamberlin was a slippery fish.

Chapter 44

The City of San Jose, tolerant of many things and often patient to a fault, had had enough. Baldy's was shut down for multiple health, fire and licensing violations. The liquor license was suspended, and, facing large fines and major costs of compliance, Baldy filed for bankruptcy and retired to the Nevada desert.

It seemed the Bigs blamed me for the demise of their clubhouse and perhaps held a grudge about my role in the downfall of their leader. As I was heading for my car in underground parking near my office one evening, the thugs came up behind me. They were not light-footed; I heard them approaching and turned around.

Sally had taught me that goons like these three were rarely in good shape, nor were they trained fighters. They had probably gotten along since adolescence on size—more fat than muscle—as well as ruthlessness and willingness to take punishment. She was right. They were also slow.

I heard Sally's voice in my head. *If you have to fight, do not hesitate, do not hold back.* As soon as they were in range, I swept Big's legs out from under him with my right leg, then kicked him in the side of his head with my left. Bigger, lagging a step behind, stumbled over him and met my right uppercut with his jaw.

I had no time to appreciate the crunching sound of his jaw or worry about the pain in my hand. Biggest was moving around his fallen comrades. I backed away until I bumped into a concrete pillar. Biggest charged. I was tempted to shout *olé* as I stepped out of his way, simultaneously using both hands to push his back forward and down. His head hit the concrete pillar. He bounced back, turned to face me, roared in anger and pain, and I kicked him in the groin as though I were attempting a game-winning 50-yard field goal in the Super Bowl. Biggest doubled over and I hit him with a solid right cross. He went down with a thud and stayed down.

Compared to Bubba, the Bigs had been lumbering walruses. They were conscious but groping around in pain as I drove away.

My hands hurt like hell.

* * *

One thing had become clear to me: if you wanted to go on a crime spree, do them in different jurisdictions.

MPD would never reopen Suzy Lou's case. It was a regrettable accident, the result of excessive partying. These things happened from time to time on Maui's

Final Part

hazardous roads. Besides, the supposed killer was already dead in California.

SJPD had the Stephanie Cunningham case; the airport was their turf. But the consensus was to put it on the back burner. Billy Mayfair probably did kill her, but maybe Dell Chamberlin was culpable as well. San Jose would see how the Chamberlin trial went.

The Santa Clara County Sheriff's Department had jurisdiction over Lexington Reservoir, where the Mayfairs drowned. But everyone agreed that Stephanie had murdered Sharon and Tommy Mayfair with no assistance from Dell Chamberlin. That case was closed.

OPD allowed that they would reopen the Billy Mayfair overdose case if Dell Chamberlin was convicted of his murder. The Santa Clara County DA pointed out to Oakland that this was circular reasoning. Calling Billy Mayfair's death a drug overdose supported Dell's defense. If Oakland, where the death occurred, called it an overdose, what was Santa Clara County doing calling it murder?

NYPD had no interest in investigating the theoretical disappearance of Graham Westonovic in an equally theoretical and uncertain timeframe. They found the idea of looking for his body in New York's vast garbage dumps months later hysterical.

Regardless, the Santa Clara County DA had inherited this mess from the occasionally joint investigation by SJPD and the Sheriff's Department. And I had gotten Dell Chamberlin to confess to his role, as well as explain how the pieces fit together.

Chapter 45

Detective Nguyen called late Friday. "They just had a hearing on the admissibility of the confession. The judge ruled it was inadmissible. More, she said any charge regarding Billy Mayfair's death should be brought in Oakland where his body was found."

The judge said that, because the recording device was Dell's property, the police had illegally searched it. Seizing it was okay, it was evidence at a crime scene. The mistake was listening to it without a warrant. They should have recorded my conversation with Dell on their own device, the 'wear a wire' thing.

"It was our mistake, Joe," she said. "But I'm afraid it gets worse. Chamberlin claims that he had been considering engaging you to work for him on an important case."

"Which was true."

"Right. And since it would be your first time working for him, he hired an agent to check you out. Gave the guy the recording device at his request, not knowing he would plant it in your office. Chamberlin claims when he learned about it, he went to your office to retrieve his property."

"Bullshit."

"It also turns out that Chamberlin has a concealed carry permit for the gun. He claims your alarm went off first and startled him, which was why he drew the weapon. He threatened to file a lawsuit claiming civil rights violations, police misconduct, and on and on unless all charges were dropped. Bottom line, the DA caved."

"But I can testify to the confession."

"Forget it, Joe. The DA won't touch this case. She said there's no hard evidence connecting Chamberlin to any of it, we can't find the money, Oakland won't budge on Billy Mayfair, and she's not willing to try to make a case on your testimony alone, not after this last clusterfuck."

"You mean he just gets away with it?"

"So it seems. Sorry, Joe. Shit happens."

* * *

"If all you're going to do is mope around, I'm going food shopping."

It was a Saturday. Anna and I should have been out doing whatever together, getting fresh air and sunshine. But I just didn't feel like it. I was, as my mom would call it, acting like a lump.

"What do we need?"

Final Part

"Everything," Anna said.

"That narrows it down."

"It's time for us to eat more healthy, economical meals."

"Okay."

"That means preparing more food at home." Anna was referring to the condo as home more and more these days. Not that I minded, but Anna had not yet officially moved in. Maybe this was the start of that conversation.

"Like frozen pizza instead of ordering in?"

"No, you goofball. That's not preparing, that's heating."

"So what exactly are you buying?"

"Staples," she said.

"Office supplies?"

"Cute, Joe. And a lot of ingredients. You may have noticed that the fridge and pantry are kind of empty."

"What do you do with these ingredients?"

"That's where the magic happens," Anna said. "You use algorithms to combine them into tasty, nutritious dishes. Only these algorithms are called recipes."

"Huh! And you can do that?"

"I can," Anna said. "You remember how we trapped Janice Sheltenham, asking her about recipes and ingredients."

"I do, and it was your brilliant idea."

"Yes, it was. Anyway, I'll be back later. You rest up

and get ready to lug packages."

Anna returned two hours later. I lugged. Anna would not let me put things away. She knew how she wanted the fridge and pantry organized, even the new spice rack she'd bought. I was clueless. Wherever there was space worked for me.

Anna was staking out and marking her territory.

* * *

We sat together on the love seat, a new living room addition. I was pooped. Anna seemed energized.

"Okay, Joe, enough ass-dragging. I know it sucks that Dell got off, but you have to let go."

I gave her a look. "Uh-oh. I know that look. You're thinking about what Spenser and Elvis Cole would do."

I changed to my 'you got me' face.

"They would both stay on the case until the balance of justice in the universe was restored," she said.

I nodded.

"All the bad guys are dead, except Dell," Anna said. "But he didn't kill the Mayfairs or Suzy Lou, and they were the only innocent victims. Graham and Stephanie and Billy were criminals. Dell was responsible for the deaths of bad guys."

"I know that," I said. *But still...*

"I have an idea," Anna said. "It might even make you feel better."

Final Part

* * *

Suzy Lou's mother was puzzled by exactly who I was, but when I said I wanted to give her and her husband an update about their daughter, she invited me to come over.

Anna and I were seated in a cozy, understated living room, with a few Chinese accessories. "I'm a private investigator. A case of mine sort of intersected with your daughter's death. I want you to know that Suzy was murdered. The woman who killed her was named Stephanie Cunningham. I say was, because she too is dead."

The couple looked quizzically at each other. It was a lot to take in. "Not an accident?" Mr. Lou said.

"No, though it was made to look like one."

"Why, Mr. Brink?"

"Your daughter was an innocent victim. She was in the wrong place at the wrong time and saw something she shouldn't have. I doubt she even knew its significance."

"Who is this Stephanie Cunningham?"

"She was a criminal. She was murdered by another criminal. I'm afraid I'm not at liberty to go into details."

But I could tell that Mr. and Mrs. Lou did not need any more details. My hope was that I had given them a semblance of closure.

Phil Bookman

Anna was right. I did feel better. That evening, we used some of those ingredients of hers to prepare a very nice meal.

Chapter 46

Dell Chamberlin was a free man. The bar association, ever protective of their own kind, had decided no disciplinary action was called for. He was a fellow lawyer, falsely accused by overzealous law enforcement. It could happen to any of them.

However, his legal practice was struggling. Dell's exoneration was great for the reputation of the lawyer who had gotten him off, but clients shied away from a criminal defense attorney who had managed to get himself arrested for murder. Dell needed money, and he needed to rebuild his reputation.

The reputation part was a funny thing. Dell was in the criminal defense business. No one wanted to deal with a criminal defense attorney until they needed one. Many law firms avoided the whole distasteful business by farming out a case when a client needed bare-knuckled criminal defense, often to a small practice like Dell's, where your effectiveness in keeping a client out of jail, or getting a minimum sentence, mattered more than anything else. In fact, an unseemly reputation could be an asset. Or so Dell had thought.

Phil Bookman

He was wrong. The taint of his arrest had, at least temporarily, put him in the penalty box. Dell knew that he would claw his way back, he had done so before, but it would take time.

Money should have been no problem, but it was. He had five million dollars parked, in fact hidden, overseas, out of the reach of the IRS and U.S. law enforcement. However, Dell was not interested in keeping his nest egg safely growing offshore to fund his retirement. His dilemma was how to get the money back into the United States where he could use it. Now. Without attracting the tax man or banking authorities who monitor inflows from foreign sources and might wonder at the source of the funds. He knew that was the one evidentiary link to the Mayfair mess that could still come back to haunt him.

The answer came unexpectedly, from a new client with a rather simple legal problem.

* * *

George Chen sat in Dell's office, across the desk from him. "How can I help you, Mr. Chen?"

"I was referred to you a few months ago by Joe Brink. He said he worked for you and you could help me with my problem. I'm afraid I didn't act immediately, but now it can't wait."

Brink! Must have made the referral before the shit

hit the fan. No need to mention that. Let's see what the kid wants

"When I was a student at the University of Arizona, I was arrested for armed robbery in this little desert town. It was a case of mistaken identity. Actually, it was more like racial profiling. Anyway, Joe Brink proved that I was 30 miles away at the time the crime was committed, and I was released.

"The thing is, my startup company is about to go live, and then we plan to file for an IPO. As a founder and officer of the company, I need to attest that I have no criminal record, which I have done. But I don't want this Arizona thing to come back and bite me in the ass in the future, so I was trying to get something official in writing from them to show that the arrest was a mistake. Just in case I ever need it. My requests were ignored. That's when Joe said it was a legal matter and I should talk to a lawyer. Then I procrastinated..."

Dell figured a phone call and a letter would take care of this, something his paralegal could do in a few minutes. "These things can be tough, but I'm sure I can clear it up for you."

George Chen smiled. "That's a relief. As you can imagine, I have a lot of other things on my plate right now."

After Dell got the details he needed from Chen, he asked, "Tell me about your company."

"I'm under extreme nondisclosure, so I can't say

much until after we announce. But it has to do with blockchain technology."

Dell was no tech expert, but he knew blockchain, whatever the hell that was, was hot. "What's your role in the company?"

"I'm chief technology officer."

That figures for an Asian guy. "I'm always interested in a good investment," Dell said.

"I think our CEO has just about closed this round. He's been great at getting investments from people who have cash stashed overseas."

"How's that work?"

"Don't ask me. I'm the tech guy, not the financial guy. I just know that he has a way for people to invest money they have stuck outside the country for some reason." He shrugged. "I think it has something to do with a loophole in the financial reporting system."

"I'd like to talk to your CEO."

George Chen looked alarmed. "He's an awfully busy guy. I probably said too much already, but I'll give him your card and tell him what you said."

"Can you at least tell me his name?"

"That I can do. It's Will. Will Graham."

* * *

Dell's work kept him on the periphery of the Silicon Valley tech industry. Sure, tech workers got involved in

Final Part

crime like everyone else, everything from DUIs, drugs and domestic violence to rape, murder and all manner of white collar crime. But criminal defense attorneys were like dentists who did root canals. You only came to them when you absolutely had too. Dell was by no means a tech insider, did not travel in the circles of those who funded and started these wonderous companies. He was no more comfortable or acceptable in their circles than an auto mechanic, maybe less so.

Like many in Silicon Valley, Dell yearned to strike it rich in the tech industry. He knew that getting in on the ground floor of a hot IPO was the only way he would ever do it. He also knew that you had to be an insider and invest before the public offering at a pre-IPO stock price, then just watch your money multiply as the post-IPO suckers piled in, bidding up the stock price in a desperate effort to get a piece of the bonanza.

And, if Chen was right, he could double his pleasure by getting his offshore hoard back home. He was desperate for spendable money. He could sell some of the stock after the public offering and relieve his financial stress.

Dell really wanted to talk to this Will Graham. But three days passed, and he heard nothing from him.

He checked out Chen. Sure enough, he was working on his doctorate at Stanford in quantum computing, whatever the hell that was.

Dell knew that most tech startups operated in

stealth mode, keeping everything as secret as possible for fear that someone would steal their brilliant idea and beat them to market. That was what Chen meant when he said he was under extreme nondisclosure. He even refused to provide the name and address of his employer on Dell's client intake form. But he did fill in a phone number.

Dell, the trial lawyer who persuaded juries, believed that he could convince anyone of anything if he could just talk to them. He called the number and got a receptionist. He asked for Mr. Graham, said it was concerning a legal matter related to George Chen. He was told that Mr. Graham was unavailable but would get the message.

He learned one thing from the call. The receptionist had answered with the company name. He'd had her spell it for him: ChainQ.

* * *

The call came in just after 5 p.m.

"Thank you for returning my call, Mr. Graham."

"George says you already took care of that little problem for him."

The guy gets right to the point. "I did."

"Look, Mr. Chamberlin, I'm awfully busy. If you took care of it, why the call?"

"I need a half-hour of your time. I think it would be

worth your while."

"You and a lot of other people. Sorry, I just can't fit you in."

Better just go for it! "I understand that you're completing your pre-IPO round. I can help you do that."

There was a pause, then: "Look, I'm meeting some investors for dinner tonight at the San Jose Fairmont. I can give you 15 minutes if you meet me in the lobby bar at 6:30."

"I'll be there."

Chapter 47

After he hung up, Dell realized he had no idea how he would identify Will Graham. He looked him up online, found several William Grahams, but none whom he thought would likely be a tech startup CEO. He would just have to wing it.

Dell walked into the Fairmont's glittering marble lobby a few minutes early and scanned the busy, sunken lounge area. There were just two men who were sitting alone. One of them looked Indian and was working on a laptop. Dell did not think Will Graham sounded like an Indian name, so he approached the other man, a white guy who was deep in conversation on his phone. As he walked up, the man looked up and they made eye contact. Dell handed him his business card and Will Graham nodded, motioned for him to have a seat, then held up one finger to signal that he was almost finished with his phone call.

Graham ended his call. The men shook hands and agreed it would be Will and Dell. Will extracted a folded document from his attaché case and handed it to Dell. "You need to sign this before we talk."

Final Part

Dell scanned the document. It was a boilerplate non-disclosure agreement. With few exceptions, Dell could not disclose or make use of information he received about ChainQ unless and until that information was made public. Dell knew that these NDAs were signed by the hundreds, maybe even the thousands, all over the Valley every day. He took a pen out of his suit jacket pocket, signed and dated the document, and handed it to Will, who put it in his attaché case and closed it.

The lobby lounge at the Fairmont had comfortable table and chair groupings spaced far enough apart that, along with the background noise from the hotel lobby, enabled the men to have a private conversation. They leaned in towards each other.

Will locked eyes with Dell and said, "The problem with blockchain is that it's not scalable. It's slow and consumes a lot of energy. Our proprietary, patented technology marries quantum computing with blockchain to overcome these barriers. ChainQ provides responsive, scalable, energy-efficient blockchain infrastructure that will be as important and widely used as the Internet itself."

Clearly, Will Graham assumed that Dell had done his homework. Dell had just gotten Will's elevator pitch, without any preamble. Dell didn't understand it but felt like he should have if only he wasn't so out of the loop on the latest technology. It sure sounded impressive.

A cocktail waitress came over, but Will waived her off and glanced at his watch. Dell got the message. Time was running out for him to make his pitch.

"I understand that you are in the last stages of completing your final funding round before filing for an IPO. I also heard that you know how to repatriate offshore funds. I have five million dollars outside the country I'd like to invest with you."

Will nodded. "Yeah. They sort of don't notice when the investment funds come from offshore, then, poof, you own U.S. stock registered at your U.S. address. Helps some of my Asian investors. But I already have commitments for all 50 million for the final round. In fact, I'm meeting with a couple of my investors in a few minutes. I'm afraid you're a bit late to the party."

Dell was crestfallen, and it showed. "I'll tell you what, Dell," Graham said. "I'm going to hold onto your card. Anything can happen when push comes to shove in a funding round. Sometimes, investors back out, usually because they can't come up with the cash when it's due. If anything becomes available, I'll let you know."

Will looked up in the direction of the entrance to the restaurant. He abruptly stood. "Sorry, I have to go now."

Dell turned his head to follow Will's back as Will strode off. Will approached two men who stepped out of the shadows in front of the restaurant to greet him.

Final Part

Dell recognized them as two of Silicon Valley's movers-and-shakers, billionaire tech mogul Mike Gold and financial wizard Nick Marchetti. They must be the investors Will was meeting. Dell knew they were way out of his league, but they sure gave Will Graham and ChainQ credibility.

Dell signaled to the cocktail waitress and ordered a double scotch. He had come so damn close...

* * *

Dell climbed out of a dead sleep with only one goal: make that goddamn noise stop. He had fallen off the wagon last night and taken a cab home. Now he had a hangover to end all hangovers.

The noise turned out to be coming from his cell phone, happily chiming to announce an incoming call. Dell reached for it on his nightstand, knocked it to the floor, felt around in the dark, and finally picked the phone up. His head felt like it was going to explode, but before he could silence the damn thing he saw both the time, 6:11 a.m., and the caller ID, Will Graham.

"Will?"

"Listen, Dell, I have an opportunity for you, but I need your answer right away."

"What..."

"I just got off the phone with Goldman. They were planning on taking us out at $10-$12. Now they want to go out at $16-$18. Which is great, but it means I need the last VC round to be $75 million instead of $50 million. So I'm raising the additional $25 million today. If you can wire the funds before noon New York time, you're in."

Dell fought to focus. Goldman must be Goldman Sachs, the premier Wall Street investment bank. If they were taking ChainQ public, it was a sure thing. And they wanted to increase the offering price. Better yet! Joy, fueled by greed, competed with misery in Dell's head. Joy won. "Count me in."

"Great. I'll email you the wire instructions. But the funds have to reach the account no later than nine o'clock Pacific time."

Right. Three-hour time difference. That's why Will's calling so early, it's just after nine now in New York.

"It'll happen. Thanks, Will."

"I'll also email you the paperwork for the stock purchase. You're a lawyer, you know the drill. There's a shitload of paper, mostly boilerplate. You need to print it, initial each page, sign where indicated, and get your signatures notarized. Then use my messenger to get it right to me. His number will be in the email. He'll be waiting for you to call, I need that by nine, too."

"Will do."

Fifteen minutes later, Dell was in his car heading for his office and its high-speed printer. He called and woke up his secretary, who was the office notary, and

Final Part

told her he needed her in early, as in right away.

Dell Chamberlin had a lot to get done in the next two hours.

* * *

Dell made the deadline. Barely.

A few minutes after nine o'clock Pacific Time, noon Eastern Time, as he sat a bit dazed in his office, the door burst open. Three men wearing dark blue windbreakers emblazoned with FBI in large yellow letters piled in. Two had weapons drawn.

"Please keep your hands on the desk where I can see them. Dell Chamberlin, we have a warrant to search these premises. A similar warrant is being executed at your home."

Dell wisely did not reach into his desk for his handgun. Moments later, he was read his rights and taken into custody.

This time, Dell Chamberlin would not wiggle out on a technicality.

* * *

The end-game started with a message left with my anonymous online phone service.

"Mr. Spenser? My name's Graham Westonovic. I understand you were looking for me a while back." He had

Phil Bookman

left a phone number.
   What the hell?

Chapter 48

earlier in the year

She saw the guy dump something in the dumpster. Her dumpster, on her turf. Just a few yards from the big carton that was her home.

She hauled whatever it was out onto the ground. Unwrapped it. Called 9-1-1. Reported the location of the body. Did not identify herself.

Then she put her stuff in her shopping cart. Time to find a new home. Maybe near one of those beaches in Brooklyn.

She was long gone when the ambulance arrived.

* * *

It was just another rollicking night at the perpetually overwhelmed South Bronx ER. By 3 a.m., the leading whiteboard candidate for the nightly "high point" *award was the morbidly obese Jane Doe who had come alone through the ER door and collapsed as it closed behind her. She remained conscious but immobile.*

She looked to be about five-foot-four and must have weighed well over 200 pounds. Deciding how to move her was delayed until the triage nurse could determine what exactly was wrong. The obstacle she presented to those exiting and entering the ER just added to the general chaos.

The woman babbled in a language none of the staff could identify, let alone understand. She kept repeating one word in particular. Although the staff spoke over a dozen languages at least well enough to treat ER patients, no one understood what the woman was saying. Was it her name?

The answer was provided by a woman accompanying another ER patient. "I think it's Slavic," she said. "I think diet'a *means baby."*

An hour later, through the efforts of four of the burliest on-duty staff who could be found, the woman was gently lifted onto one of the hospitals heavy-duty wheeled beds and moved to an OR, where she promptly gave birth to healthy twin girls by C-Section.

Who she was and how she had gotten to the ER were yet to be determined.

The "low point" entry on the whiteboard was four-

Final Part

year-old LaTasha Williams. LaTasha had been sent outside to sit on the front stoop with her dolly while her mother entertained her boyfriend. Sometime after midnight, gunshots were heard by neighbors, but that was not uncommon in the gang-ridden neighborhood, and no one was foolish enough to investigate. If the frolicking couple heard the shots, they too had ignored them.

LaTasha was found—more like, tripped over—by the boyfriend when he left around 1 a.m. Loverboy anonymously called 9-1-1 without informing the mother of his discovery and split.

The little girl was almost gone when she arrived in the ER. Despite heroic efforts, at least partially fueled by outrage, her tiny body finally succumbed.

LaTasha had been an innocent victim of a stray shot in a drive-by shooting, as well as parental neglect and indifference. Indignant NYPD cops from the local precinct were taking this case personally.

Given those leading candidates for the night's high and low points—and the night was still young—the John Doe who was brought in after a homeless woman found him wrapped in a tarp in a dumpster was just another urban ER case.

* * *

The immediate problem was the bullet wound in John

Doe's head. It had been a through-and-through, which was a lucky thing, if you can call anything about such a shooting lucky. When a bullet bounces around inside a skull, it turns the brain to mush. The patient's brain was still functioning well enough to keep him alive. The life-threatening aspect of this wound was the loss of blood.

John Doe had very nearly bled out. But, since he was still alive, that was a problem they could fix. As his body refilled with blood, some of John Doe's other wounds began to bleed again. They were an impressive and disturbing array. Wounds were cleaned. Sutures were applied. At least nothing appeared to have been broken. His abuser was a cutter, not a cracker or crusher.

Except, that is, for his face. It had been savagely beaten and broken.

"What could have done this?" the shocked intern asked the resident, who had come in to check on the patient.

"I'd say our guy had been methodically tortured over at least several hours, maybe even days. There was a personal element, destroying his face that way, especially since he was going to kill him. Sadistic. Then he was executed, however unsuccessfully. But none of that goes in the chart. Just the facts using medical terminology."

Stabilized, John Doe was transferred to the ICU

Final Part

where neurology would take over. How much of his mind the bullet had left behind was not the ER's problem.

Chapter 49

"For all we have learned about it, the brain is fundamentally a mystery," the neurologist said.

After surgically cleaning things up as best they could, and treating the festering wound in the patient's foot, neurology had put John Doe in a medically-induced coma. This was done to give the injured parts of the brain time to heal without the stress of much stimulation to handle. It also prevented the brain from attempting to heal itself by depriving wounded tissue of nourishment, killing damaged tissue and redirecting resources to healthy tissue. It was one of many situations in which a biological strategy developed over eons of evolution was in conflict with the interventions of modern medicine.

Meanwhile, the oral and maxillofacial surgeon had gone to work, essentially rebuilding the patient's face. The beating had spared his eyes, but his nose, checks, mouth and jaw were decimated. Multiple surgeries were required. With no "before" picture, they did the best they could, but it was unlikely the man would look like he had previously. Another thing for the poor man

Final Part

to cope with when he woke up.

Now, many weeks later, they had brought him out of the coma. He was conscious. His vital signs and neurological responses were good. He was bright eyed, alert and made good eye-contact. He seemed to understand oral communication. He just did not communicate back. After some trial and error, they had gotten him to hold up one finger for yes, two fingers for no. It was a start.

The neurologist continued. "Do you know your name?"

2 fingers.

"Do you know why you're here?"

2 fingers.

"You were shot in the head. You almost died."

No change in affect. Still good eye-contact and an engaged, pleasant smile.

"Does that upset you?"

1 finger, then 2 fingers.

"Yes and no?"

1 finger.

The oral and maxillofacial surgeon took over. "Your face was badly beaten. Fixing that was my job, and it's pretty much healed, though your jaw may be sore until you start using it more. Would you like to see what you look like?"

1 finger.

They held a mirror in front of him. He turned his

head from side-to-side. No change of affect.

"Do you like what you see?"

1 finger, then 2 fingers.

"Do you look like you remember?"

No response.

"Do you remember what you looked like?"

2 fingers.

The doctors had no interest in crime-solving. One was interested in how his patient's brain was working. The other, if he had created an acceptable face. A nurse whispered something, and the neurologist asked one last question, one that simply hadn't occurred to her, but was certainly worth verifying.

"Is English your preferred language?"

1 finger.

"Well then, good enough for now. Since you don't know your name and you had no ID, you've become one of our John Does. But that seems too impersonal now, so the staff have decided to call you Lucky, at least until your real identity is established. Is that okay with you?"

1 finger.

* * *

NYPD Detective Julio Ramsey had run his victim's fingerprints and DNA through the FBI's national database. Given the medical report of the condition of his

Final Part

body and where it was found, Ramsey had been confident he would be in the system. He was sure it was a bad-guy-on-bad-guy crime. He was astonished when the results came back negative. No hit. Not even a close match.

There was nothing much else to investigate. The anonymous 9-1-1 call had come in on a prepaid, unregistered phone. The scuzzy area in which the victim was found yielded no useful evidence. The old tarp only confirmed that the victim had been wrapped in it. There was no clothing to reveal clues; other than the tarp, the patient had been naked.

Detective Ramsey checked with missing persons. There was no match to any of their open cases, but they would let him know if any report matching his victim came in.

Meanwhile, it went on Ramsey's back-burner, there to wait for a development, like the victim remembering something.

* * *

Lucky was transferred to the hospital's rehab unit. The therapies began. Occupational therapy, physical therapy and speech therapy to start. Cognitive therapy, the care team decided, would wait a while. No need to overload Lucky's still-healing brain.

His deficits were as random as the path the bullet

had taken. For example, he could dress himself just fine, but was flummoxed by fasteners, be they buttons, zippers, buckles, whatever. He could walk okay, but his left leg occasionally struck out on its own. Except for the manual dexterity, OT and PT for these sorts of things proceeded well. He relearned. His muscle tone improved rapidly.

Speech therapy stalled until an OT discovery caused a breakthrough. Though he had difficulty holding a writing instrument, with effort, Lucky could and would write answers to questions. However, he could not read what he wrote. But when it was read to him, he replied with one finger. Yes.

He was supplied with a tablet—he could tap out answers using the onscreen keyboard—and communication began in earnest. It was quickly established that Lucky's personal memories began with waking up in the ICU. His general long-term memory seemed intact. History, like who is the president, what year is it, those sorts of memories were normal enough. But not things like what city are you in? Where do you live? What kind of work do you do? These drew a reply of "no idea."

Another week, another breakthrough. Reading started to come back. In a few days, Lucky could read aloud like a normal adult. Just read though, not ask or answer questions, but he had a voice, and a rather

Final Part

pleasant one at that. Another week, and he was tapping out questions, not just answers. The icon cards for things like bathroom, water and other simple needs were no longer needed.

Then one day he asked the speech therapist, aloud, "What is my part?" It was the last piece of the communication puzzle. Lucky was officially talking.

Versions of that specific question about his part were often asked and had the care team stumped. True, he asked other questions about himself that they could not answer, and they told him he would have to wait for his memory to return. But this business about a part was a puzzling obsession.

Given his other progress, they were confident most of Lucky's memory would eventually return, except perhaps, as often was the case, the events immediately preceding the gunshot. PT, OT and speech therapy were no longer needed. Cognitive therapy was never started. Other than not knowing his personal history, Lucky had recovered remarkably.

It was time to discharge him, but to where? He was an unidentified, able-bodied, healthy man with amnesia. His assigned social worker decided on a Friday to discuss alternatives with Lucky the following Monday. She wanted the weekend to narrow down the alternatives to a short list.

* * *

Phil Bookman

On Monday, Lucky pre-empted the social worker. He had remembered a few things over the weekend. He knew he was from California and was visiting New York to perform his part.

"Your part in what, Lucky?"

"I don't know yet, but it'll come to me. And my name isn't Lucky. It's Billy Graham."

Chapter 50

"Is he nuts?"

"No, detective, there is no evidence of mental disease or defect. He just has residual amnesia secondary to a brain injury."

Detective Julio Ramsey scratched his head. The doctor, wearing a white robe, looked impatient to get out of her tiny hospital office. She had patients to see.

"Just to be clear, doc. You have no grounds to hold him? Like, because he's delusional?"

"A delusion is a belief that is demonstrably false. Just because he thinks his name is Billy Graham does not make him delusional. Yes, a very famous old preacher named Billy Graham died last year. But I'm told it isn't an uncommon name. In fact, I once went to a concert in San Francisco at Bill Graham Auditorium, named after a rock music promotor.

"Just because no one can find a record of our Billy Graham does not mean that's not his name. Our patient has no religious delusions, does not think he is this famous preacher, he just thinks he's finally remembered his name. And even if he's wrong, that's not *a delusion, just an incorrect memory.*

"The patient is physically and mentally fit to leave. In fact, he needs to leave. I've already written his discharge orders."

The doctor did not go into the patient's complete and rather complicated medical condition in detail; only his mental state was relevant to the conversation.

Detective Ramsey had spoken with his victim less than an hour before. He had no memory of why he had been beaten, shot and left for dead, or by whom, nothing to help the investigation. And he had no idea who he was except for this Billy Graham thing.

"We have no legal grounds to hold him, either," the exasperated detective said. "Once he leaves here, he's free to go anywhere."

"That's what freedom is all about, Detective."

* * *

Before Detective Ramsey could connect with him one last time, Billy Graham was gone. The little party, complete with cake and punch, was over. The staff at the hospital had chipped in for some clothing, toiletries and a small wheeled suitcase, and tears were shed.

His social worker had gotten him, at his request, a bus ticket to San Jose, California—another memory cell had fired—and enough pocket money to last the

Final Part

trip with a few bucks left over. She gave him a sheet listing the various human services agencies he could make use of when he arrived in San Jose and made sure he understood that he should get into treatment as soon as he arrived. They had even issued him a temporary but official photo ID—it looked just like a driver's license—in the name of William Graham. All of this was a cheap yet legitimate way for New York to punt this already monumentally expensive and uninsured medical patient west.

Left with no alternative, Detective Ramsey closed the police case. At no time had anything about a Graham Westonovic come his way.

* * *

The three-and-a-half-day bus trip to San Jose was interrupted when he got off in Indianapolis. His amnesia had begun to recede more rapidly on the bus. He now knew his real name was Graham Westonovic. He also knew his part was, or had been, to play Billy Mayfair, though exactly why and what that entailed were still a blank. It amused him that his addled brain had blended the two names together and come up with this famous Billy Graham character. It was such a Hollywood sort of thing to do.

Hollywood. Acting. More dormant brain cells had awakened.

Phil Bookman

He knew Indianapolis was his hometown. It was where he could get some of the answers he needed to learn his history and make sense of the last several months.

Getting shot in the head and left for dead tends to make you cautious. He knew he needed someone he could trust to help him. He sensed that much of his family might not meet that standard. He was not sure why he felt that way, but he trusted the strong feeling.

When Graham Westonovic, a.k.a. William Graham, got off the bus in Indianapolis, he went looking for Aunt Hilda.

* * *

The Westonovic clan had, for generations, employed two defenses against unacceptable behavior by one of its members. The first was denial. They did not speak of it; therefore it did not exist.

This was how the horrid rumors that came from California about Stephanie being involved in murders were handled. The poor thing was dead. Her body had been returned to her widowed mother Hilda in Indianapolis for burial in the family plot. The family had mourned. The unpleasantness was never mentioned.

The second Westonovic defense mechanism, employed much less frequently, was ostracism. This was

Final Part

used for those who continued their unacceptable behavior. The offender was ejected from the clan as if he or she had never existed, never to be contacted or spoken of again. It was this shunning that had been used to deal with Graham Westonovic's abhorrent homosexuality. It was a stricture cousin Stephanie had rejected.

* * *

"Hello, Aunt Hilda. It's me. Graham."

Hilda Westonovic looked with confusion, then astonishment at the man standing on her doorstep. "Graham? Oh my god, it is you. What happened to your face?"

"It's a long story. May I come in?"

"Of course."

She lived alone. She could put Graham up for a while and the rest of the family wouldn't know. But only for a short while.

Chapter 51

"So, you're really Joe Brink, not Cole Spenser?"

I grinned. "So, you're really Graham Westonovic, not Graham West or Billy Graham?"

It was Graham's turn to smile. "Don't forget, I was almost Billy Mayfair, too."

We were sitting in my office. It was a week after that first call. Since then, we'd spoken by phone every day. Now we were finally meeting face-to-face. Speaking of faces, I could barely recognize the guy sitting across from me from his old photos. I said so.

"Billy Mayfair beat the crap out of my face. Really broke it up. The doctors reconstructed it, but they didn't know what I looked like before."

"Well, you look okay, just different. Sort of ruggedly handsome."

"I know," Graham said. "I used to be a pretty boy. But that's the least of my worries."

"ALS?" I said. He had told me about that, and a lot more, during our phone conversations.

"Amyotrophic lateral sclerosis. Lou Gehrig's disease. Like I told you, they found it when they were

Final Part

treating my head injury. Aunt Hilda confirmed it's what killed my uncle in his 50s. Mine seems to have shown up even earlier. It runs in the family on the male side. Not everyone gets it, but we're probably all carriers. The thing is, the way the Westonovic family works, no one ever spoke of it. My uncle's death was treated as some sort of a mystery illness. But I think my grandad died the same way."

Seeing Graham, who looked just fine, and hearing about his terminal illness in person was sobering. I didn't know what to say. Graham filled the void.

"I told you about the bullet, right? Who knew you could live without part of your brain?"

"You've made an amazing recovery."

"So they tell me. My memory seems to be mostly back. It's a funny thing how that happens. It's like looking for a document where you know you filed it, only it's not there. Later, you look in the same place for it, and there it is. That's how my memory has returned. I don't have to work at it, just let it happen. Although sometimes I wonder if memory is such a good thing."

"I guess we all have things we'd prefer to forget," I said.

"You're telling me. Just so you know where I'm coming from, I know Stevie and I had planned some horrendous, unforgivable stuff. I don't know about her, but I remember treating it like some sort of part to play, like it wasn't real. I think I spent a lot of my life doing that sort of thing. It worked well for me up until I was supposed to kill Billy Mayfair, which I couldn't do in real life, and you know where that got me."

I thought about how Stephanie had manipulated Graham. To him, she was always cousin Stevie, his friend and confidant, looking out for him. To her, he was an actor, taking direction.

"Anyway, they say I have a 50-50 chance to live two more years. Almost no chance of making it to five years. I barely have any symptoms yet, just some fine motor trouble with buttons, using a mouse, that sort of thing. But they tell me that's going to change soon and then I'll go downhill fast. Sometimes it sucks to have such a precise prognosis."

I had nothing to say about that, either.

"Knowing you're dying sharpens your focus. I'm ready to take my punishment for the part I played in the Mayfair murders. But first I want to get that Dell Chamberlin bastard."

"About you facing charges, unless you hold a news conference and confess, there won't be any. They have no evidence that ties you directly to the Mayfair murders. As far as they're concerned, Stephanie and Billy were in cahoots on that. Case closed. I also had a hypothetical conversation with a Public Defender I know. She then had a hypothetical conversation with someone in the DA's office. Bottom line is that no one would be interested in prosecuting someone who is dying

Final Part

from ALS. The exact quote was, 'It would look mean-spirited and be a waste of taxpayer dollars.'"

Graham laughed. "I think I can keep my mouth shut about it."

"What say we focus on getting Dell Chamberlin?" I said.

"Joe, you can't imagine what it was like sitting in that warehouse, cold, naked, starving, beat up and tortured, hearing him calmly tell Billy step-by-step how to kill me and get rid of my body. Then he explained to him how they were going to rip off the Mayfair's money after Stevie killed them." Graham shut his eyes and slowly shook his head. "I know I treated Stevie's plan like the Mayfair's weren't real people, but hearing those two talking so cold-blooded about killing me and Billy's parents made me realize how crazy Stevie and I had been. And I'm sure Dell Chamberlin had Stevie killed. I can't let get him away with it."

Now I had a lot to say. "How about we get us a bag of donuts, then I'll tell you the plan I've cooked up."

"Sounds good to me. I don't have to worry about my diet anymore."

Chapter 52

After I got that first call from Graham, I contacted Detectives Nguyen and Taylor and told them I had a lead on Graham Westonovic. They both said pretty much the same thing. They didn't care. Their cases were closed and the whole mess was politically radioactive. No one was concerned any longer about Graham Westonovic or, for that matter, Dell Chamberlin.

I did not know what to do. I was flailing around when Anna suggested I talk to my financial guru, Nick Marchetti, about the money Dell had stolen and stashed offshore. Maybe, she thought, he would have an idea about how to get some government agency interested in that.

Nick is a sucker for a free lunch at Greasy Jack's, even if it's just burgers and fries. As soon as I told him about Dell's scam and my problem getting local law enforcement to pursue it, he got a big grin on his face. "I know just the man we need to talk to."

"We?"

"This sounds like it could be fun," Nick said. "If you don't mind, I'd like to help you get the guy."

Final Part

The man Nick knew turned out to be FBI Special Agent in Charge Alex Greene. Nick said that he and Alex went way back. I had also dealt with Greene before, handling some fallout from the Accidental Hero case.

"I'm sure Alex will be happy to bust this Dell Chamberlin's international money laundering scheme," Nick said. "Nabbing an infamous, bent defense lawyer trying to hide his ill-gotten gains is just the thing to get an FBI agent's juices flowing. That, and the great PR."

"How is it a money laundering scheme?" I wondered aloud.

"It isn't yet. But we can make it into one. Then we'll give it to Alex with a nice ribbon around it, maybe add a bow." Nick explained his idea.

I told Nick that it would be the third trap I had attempted to use in the Mayfair case. The first was the attempt to lure Billy Mayfair with the promise of $750,000 in insurance money. That backfired and probably got him killed. The second was setting Dell up to confess. That worked, but the cops bungled it. If only I'd worn a wire.

As always, Nick oozed confidence. "Don't worry, Joe. We'll nail the bastard."

Before he went to work as Mike Gold's chief financial officer, Nick Marchetti had been one of Silicon Valley's leading venture capitalists. Nick knew everything there was to know about funding rounds for startups, public offerings, moving money, the whole thing. Nick coached Graham and me on how to be credible and set Dell up.

"We have to get him to court Graham. Dell needs to be the yearning suitor. Graham needs to be the reluctant maiden. Dell needs to feel that he did the seducing. He needs to feel grateful, lucky that you'll finally give in and take his money, and desperate to follow your instructions to the letter. We want him to avoid asking questions because he fears doing so might scotch the deal."

I was curious about how Nick knew so much about running a financial con, but decided I might be better off not asking, never mind knowing.

I tried to get George Chen to play his part by promising I would never ask him for another favor again. It was a big ask, but George said he wouldn't mind having something officially exonerating him. He also reminded me that the debt he owed me could never be repaid. He even recruited his sister Allie to play the part of the ChainQ receptionist; she carried a burner phone, waited for Dell to call, then flawlessly did her part in conning him.

My buddy Ricky Clancy acted as Will Graham's messenger. He took a break from his Uber driving, waited nearby for Dell's call, then picked up the documents and dropped them off at the security desk at the FBI's San Jose office, attention Alex Greene.

Final Part

I was the director of the production, with George, Allie, Ricky and Graham playing their roles. Nick even got his boss and longtime buddy Mike Gold to join him in a bit part, meeting Graham for dinner at the Fairmont. Billionaire Gold was well-known and recognizable, and we figured that his appearance as an investor would wipe out any doubt Dell might have about Will Graham's bona fides.

Graham played the lead to perfection. He became the harried, focused startup CEO reluctant to take the mark's money. He learned the elevator pitch Nick crafted, with an ease that he said surprised him. Difficult memorizing lines had severely hampered his acting career. He credited the gunshot through his brain for this improvement.

I was astonished watching Graham immerse himself in what he called his final part. He learned the necessary jargon from Nick and online research. His whole demeanor seemed to undergo a transformation and his voice and body language changed when he was playing Will Graham, startup CEO. We chose the name Will Graham because it tickled him and sounded right for the part.

It was Nick's idea to create the short timeline the last day of the con. It was not unrealistic, he said. It was often how deals went, hurry up and wait until the last minute, then scramble when the Wall Street money merchants set a nearly impossible deadline. He said that they habitually ignore the time zone difference between the coasts. Even though Dell was a criminal defense attorney, Nick was sure he would have analogous deadline experience, probably driven by unreasonable judges.

What Dell did not know was that ChainQ had been set up as a sole proprietorship with Dell himself as the owner. We then opened a bank account for ChainQ with Dell as the account owner.

The plan was for Dell to wire the $5 million he had stashed offshore into that bank account thinking he was making an investment in Will Graham's startup. Instead, it would appear to be the domestic account for a U.S.-based shell company Dell was hiding behind to launder overseas funds, leaving a clear electronic and paper trail for the FBI to follow.

Operating on what was labelled an anonymous tip, an FBI agent started monitoring the ChainQ account, using the password the tipster conveniently provided. Once the wire transfer hit, the raids on Dell Chamberlin's home and office commenced.

The FBI specializes in tracing electronic financial transactions. It especially helps when they know the start and end points of the money trail. In this case, the start was Billy Mayfair's bank account, the end was ChainQ's. The FBI then tied the money movement into the evidence previously gathered against Dell by local law enforcement.

Final Part

The feds chose not to reveal how a thick packet of incriminating documents, initialed and signed by Dell Chamberlin, and duly notarized, had been delivered into their hands. It was vaguely attributed to their wondrous investigative prowess. Dell claimed he had been conned into signing them. Even his own lawyer found it hard to believe that an experienced attorney would sign such documents without first reading them.

Dell could not substantiate his fantastic story about the swindler Will Graham. No such person seemed to exist. The phone numbers Dell claimed belonged to ChainQ and Graham were those of untraceable burner phones that were never found. As for his sorry attempt to implicate George Chen, a graduate student at Stanford, George was baffled by Dell's story. He was struggling with his PhD thesis and had no time for anything else, certainly not working for a startup company. He stated that Dell had provided a simple legal service for him, clearing up that Arizona matter. George waived attorney-client privilege. Dell's own records confirmed George's account, and that they had only met once, for less than 30 minutes.

* * *

The headline in the *San Jose Mercury News* read, "Lawyer Ripped Off Estate, Laundered Millions." The article also implicated Dell in at least the murder of

Billy Mayfair and hinted at his involvement in a conspiracy involving several related murders. It was accompanied by a nice photo of FBI Special Agent in Charge Alex Greene announcing Dell Chamberlin's arrest at a press conference.

Acknowledgements

To my wife and editor, Lois, and my sister-in-law and proofreader, Judy, once more my heartfelt thanks. I appreciate your patience, precision and enthusiasm.

I also want to thank readers who take the time to write a review on Amazon. I love the feedback, and others appreciate your thoughts.

About the Author

Phil Bookman had a long career as a software entrepreneur, starting a number of successful software companies. He is now retired from the software industry, and spends much of his time writing mystery novels with Silicon Valley heroes.

Phil grew up in Seaford, New York, where he met and married his high school sweetheart, Lois. He has degrees from Rensselaer Polytechnic Institute, Adelphi University and Santa Clara University. Lois and Phil reside in Los Gatos, California and have lived in Silicon Valley since 1974.

Contact Phil at philtheauthor@outlook.com
Visit Phil's author page at philbookman.com
All Phil's books are available on Amazon.com

Also by Phil Bookman

Fiction
Joe Brink Mystery Series
Venture Capital Pie (Book 1)

Mike Gold Mystery Series
Wind and Fire (Book 11)
Santa's Village (Book 10)
Gold Moonshot (Book 9)
The Yippee Murders (Book 8)
Gold Jihad (Book 7)
Death Order (Book 6)
Alias (Book 5)
Slice (Book 4)
Riding the Tiger (Book 3)
Charisma (Book 2)
Opium (Book 1)

Non-Fiction
Attacking The Crown Jewels

Made in the USA
Middletown, DE
07 November 2023